PALETTE of *Grace*

A Collection of Short Works

Edited by
Anne Hamilton & Ruth Bonetti

Donna Albrecht   **Anne Hamilton**
Hazel Barker   **John Hughes**
Linda Barton   **Pamela Julian**
Ruth Bonetti with **Justen Wani Nasona**
Ross Clark   **Jim McPherson**
Diana Davison   **Rosemary New**
Miranda de Jager   **Judy Rogers**
M. Lester Dighton **Jo Wanmer**
Terry Gatfield   **Emely Weiler**
Lynda Hammond

Palette of Grace

Anne Hamilton, Ruth Bonetti (editors)

© Individual contributors 2024

Published by Armour Books
P. O. Box 492, Corinda QLD 4075

Cover & interior design and typeset by Beckon Creative

Images: Elvira Draat, iStock | A handmade alcohol ink painting on Yupo paper. Spectrum Sherbet Palette Transfers © 2022 Katie Pertiet and Artisan®6 textures, courtesy of Forever.com

ISBN: 978-1-925380-73-6

 A catalogue record for this book is available from the National Library of Australia

PALETTE of *Grace*

A Collection of Short Works

Edited by
Anne Hamilton & Ruth Bonetti

Contents

SECTION I – FICTION

FICTION

The Chosen Stone

ROSEMARY NEW

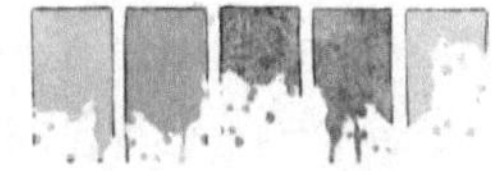

Simeon struggled from his camp stretcher, easing stiffness against tell-tale years of fossicking. He sat on the edge of the stretcher frame and held his head in his hands, while his body accustomed itself to feeling upright before he attempted to stand.

Raising his head, he stared out the hut window towards barren dirt piles scattered as far as the morning sunshine reached. How long had he been digging? Should he bother anymore? Simeon let his breath fall out in a sigh. He used to be certain that under all that dirt, it was there. It had to be! But how could he find it, when all his prospecting since that one seam ten years ago had yielded so little? It was exhausted now. Like himself. Outside, the morning heat shimmered, and he should make some effort before it got too hot. But effort required motivation and nobody could show him where to dig. Why bother?

Something deep in his soul had always urged him to keep looking. But the pain in his back told him enough was enough. He'd searched. He hadn't found.

Sighing and leaning forwards, Simeon folded his arms across his legs and looked around the hut. A sink and a table, a billy-can and a packet of tea leaves. A cup of tea might help. Beside his stretcher stood an old box with an open packet of biscuits on top. And his old King James pocket Bible. He hadn't bothered with that for a long time, either.

As Simeon reached over to grab a biscuit, he accidentally knocked the Bible off the box. It fell open onto the dirt floor. He bent over to pick it up, looking for inspiration where the book had fallen open.

'For I know the thoughts that I think toward you, saith the Lord, thoughts of peace, and not of evil, to give you an expected end. Then shall ye call upon Me, and ye shall go and pray unto Me, and I will hearken unto you. And ye shall seek Me, and find Me, when ye shall search for Me with all your heart.'

Simeon read the first line again, out loud. 'God's still thinking 'bout ME?' He pondered over this thoughtfulness of God's, then re-read the last line.

'…ye shall find Me when ye search for Me with all your heart.'

Holding the Bible open at that page, Simeon gazed around his small hut. What was he really searching for? Had God really been thinking 'bout Simeon all this time? He stared hard at that first verse again,

'…to give you an expected end.'

Simeon was wide awake now. His expected end was to find that one precious stone which was still hiding in his mining claim.

Simeon folded the corner of the page over into a dog-ear, then reverently placed the Bible back on top of the box. He reached down to where his work boots stood neatly beside the stretcher. He always pulled on his boots before he stood up. 'A man's never dressed without his boots,' he reminded himself, his voice determined as he pushed a biscuit out of the packet and crunched noisily. With boots on and laced up tight, Simeon stood to his feet, stretching his arms forwards and backwards, unlocking stiff joints. It was time to make that cup of tea.

Outside the hut, Simeon worked the hand-pump on the well to bring up cool fresh water into his billy-can, then locked the handle down and walked to his campfire, now just glowing ash from last night's cook-up. He kicked at the ash and an ember sprung to a flame, so he reached for some kindling to build it up, and hung the billy over the fire. While it simmered away, he retrieved a handful of tea leaves from the hut, throwing them into the billy to make a brew.

Simeon crouched down on one leg to watch the progress, and planned his day. 'An expected end… well, God,' he said 'I haven't said a prayer to You for longer than I can remember. But that Bible of Yours… I reckon You showed me something today. If You've been searching for me while I've been busy searching for that real special stone, would You mind showing me where I can find it today?'

Simeon poured from the boiling billy into his cup and walked inside to sit down. With a soothing cupful of strong tea, he stared absently at the faded magazine on the table. It was always open. He pulled it towards him to read the familiar article. *'A Master Craftsman,'* the headlines proclaimed. *'A Remote Location & Precious Gems.'*

Simeon smiled to himself. Although he enjoyed this solitude, he also relished that celebrity month, which gave him a strange sort of private renown, away from prying eyes and claim jumpers. The magazine had laid on his table for years, tattered and dirty from blowing about in the dusty air. He nodded at the article, like he was agreeing with it, and read the lines he knew so well, *'This old fossicker has supplied some of the best gems ever to come to market. His superior craftsmanship has quickly caught international interest in the gem and jewellery industry.'*

Simeon got up for one more biscuit, then returned to the final paragraph. *'"There's a precious stone out there,' the old man says as he laces his boots before getting off his bed, 'it's the purest, clearest jewel — it's been waiting since the world began."'*

Abruptly he pushed the magazine into a drawer under the table, and slammed it shut, declaring, 'But I'm going to find it before I die!'

Simeon swallowed the last of his tea, and tossed the empty cup into the sink. His broad smile anticipated the magazine's promise, just like that Bible said this morning, an 'expected end.' He slapped on a beaten-up hat, and walked out of the hut. Something in his heart drew him to a subsidence of the earth he had previously ignored.

Soon the old fossicker was wielding a pick. He slammed it down into the surface, again and again, until a glinting seam exposed. 'There's one or two good stones for a start today,' he muttered. Thrusting his shovel into the freshly broken clumps, he shook gravel into a sieve, then investigated closer, eyes squinting in the glare. Simeon deftly fingered through the gravel, work-toughened hands carefully assessing each stone, lifting one by one into the sunlight to rotate between his fingers. Some he dropped inside the leather pouch hanging from his belt, others he flicked onto the pile of sandy dirt, little stones cascading down in a dusty fall. Pushing a fingery track through his tray, he suddenly stopped to gather up a single stone. As he lifted it into the sunlight, a smile risked its way across his face. Simeon held onto it like life itself! He stood motionless. The pounding of his heart resounded in his ears.

The stone?

Simeon looked away over a surging sea of dirt-piles and then chanced another look.

The Stone!

Simeon felt faint in the richness of the moment. Even the landscape seemed to be swaying along with his overpowering disbelief. His hands shook, so he gripped the stone tight, and clenched securely inside the leather pouch. Simeon cried aloud, 'God! You really DO think of me!'

He tipped the tattered hat back off his forehead, knocked the sieve upside down with the edge of his boot, and returned to camp with the chosen stone safely grasped in his hand, inside the leather pouch. Through the open hut door, past the table and into the gem room. He slung the stool forwards with a well-aimed thrust of his leg, hauled it towards the bench with his free hand, and sat, leaning over. Reaching up with the same hand, he switched on the lights, carefully withdrew his fist from the pouch and slowly uncurled his fingers. Finding that the stone was still safe, Simeon lifted it out, his heart racing.

Simeon concentrated on the rough stone. It was huge, the biggest he had ever extracted throughout all his mining years. Carats! How many carats? He could barely breathe with the enormity of this scale. He rolled the stone between his fingers, under the lights, then in front of the lights. Even before beginning to cut, it flashed colours he never imagined. A sharp breath blew between his lips. He shook his head at the gift in his keeping. 'Just can't believe this…' he whispered to it. Simeon sat back and closed his eyes for a moment, then opened them again. The stone was still there. Raw beauty. He leaned forward and pulled the magnifying glass across. Simeon gazed through it, at the stone's deep, rectangular form.

He had to pause, to prepare his breath. It was going to take a good while—but he had all day, all night probably— in fact, the rest of his life if need be. The words that his Bible opened at on the floor filtered into his memory. He nodded. 'Yes, God! You really did it! You showed me where

I could find it! Guess You found me, too, like that said. Took You long enough, God. Guess both us were digging in the wrong place.'

Simeon stopped, maybe he was talking rubbish. God was God, after all.

He examined the depth and dimensions of the stone, preforming the rough gem inside his imagination. Never had he found a stone of this quality in all his lifetime. It was all he ever hoped for, and more! Faceting images began forming in his mind's eye, the Radiant Cut… absolutely! 70 perfect facets—seventy! Just like himself, 70, rough and radiant! This was going to be momentous! He reached for a new piece of wax and manipulated it between the warmth of his fingers, attached to a dop stick, mounted the stone onto the wax and located the dop into his grinding machine. Next, he needed a lap disc to commence the initial grinding away of the rough. He unwrapped a new one from its old wrapper, and laid it inside the machine.

Smiling, Simeon flicked the switch and the machine started whirring. He settled into his familiar routine, lowering the dop with the rough stone onto the lap as it whirled around. No hurry. Every few moments he lifted the dop away from the revolving lap, relocated it into a different hole on the block, and again lowered onto the lap to continue grinding the rough away. He changed laps into finer and finer grades, polishing the facets to reflective clarity. Dazzling colours refracted from the facets under the bright lights. Slowly, from the raw stone in the hands of a master craftsman emerged a precious jewel, its inner beauty now released as he pulled it off the wax for the last time and wiped it over as carefully as silk. Every way he moved it, light scattered coloured prisms around the room.

When Simeon relaxed away from the bench, he was surprised that darkness had covered the landscape. Calls of night-birds had gone unnoticed. He held the stone tightly while flicking off the lights. Sunset's last light surrendered to night.

Simeon's breath faltered. A golden haze darted and danced where he slumped. His hands opened, loosening their grip. The chosen stone dropped to the floor—where the heavenly angelic host was waiting in the mist to gather him up.

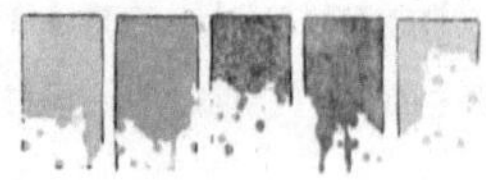

The inspiration for Simeon's character was drawn from Luke's Gospel.

Luke 2:25–30 NKJV

'And behold, there was a man in Jerusalem whose name was Simeon, and this man was just and devout, waiting for the Consolation of Israel, and the Holy Spirit was upon him. And it had been revealed to him by the Holy Spirit that he would not

see death before he had seen the Lord's Christ. So he came by the Spirit into the temple. And when the parents brought in the Child Jesus, to do for Him according to the custom of the law, he took Him up in his arms and blessed God and said: 'Lord, now You are letting Your servant depart in peace, according to Your word; for my eyes have seen Your salvation.'

Simeon the fossicker had been waiting all his life too, for the fulfilment of his own search. When he found it, he knew his gifted craftsmanship would bring a precious jewel into light.

God is the Master Craftsman! His Chosen Stone is Christ, and we come into His hands as living stones.

1 Peter 2:4–5 NKJV

Coming to Him as to a living stone, rejected indeed by men, but chosen by God and precious, you also, as living stones, are being built up a spiritual house, a holy priesthood, to offer up spiritual sacrifices acceptable to God through Jesus Christ.

God sees through our rough, raw nature, and facets us into the likeness of Christ through trials of faith, cutting away everything that does not glorify Him. Whichever way your life turns, facets in every circumstance will capture the Light of God's glory within you, refracting and radiating His Light in a multitude of directions.

Malachi 3:17 NKJV

'They shall be Mine,' says the Lord of hosts, 'On the day that I make them My jewels.'

Jeremiah 29:11–13 NKJV

'For I know the thoughts that I think toward you, says the Lord, thoughts of peace and not of evil, to give you a future and a hope. Then you will call upon Me and go and pray to Me, and I will listen to you. And you will seek Me and find Me, when you search for Me with all your heart.'

Nightwatch and the Seed Man

TERRY GATFIELD

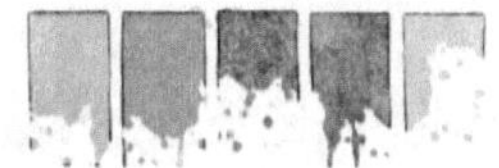

$\mathcal{I}$t was post-war London of the late 1940s. I was about six years of age living with mum and dad, two siblings and a mongrel dog named Patsy. Opposite my home was a derelict house demolished in a Luftwaffe raid. This bombed-out shell and surrounds were my playgrounds 24/7.

My evenings were very special, particularly during the winter months. At some stage a canvas-clad steel frame arrived on the footpath outside the remains of the building. Along with the frame came a kindly old man with the odd name, Dougal Brownski. His companion was an overweight German shepherd with a timidity the inverse of his size.

Several of my mates—usually numbering four—found Dougal to be a real friend. As evening approached, we would help him prepare his kerosene safety lights. He taught us everything like proper soldier cadets. Trimming the wicks, setting their correct height, cleaning the red glass lenses and filling them with kero. When ready, we would place them like guardian sentries around the danger zones of the bomb site.

When positioned, we were told to stand erect, officially salute each safety light and say out loud, 'Custodian, it is your duty and privilege to protect the neighbourhood this night.'

It was Dougal who taught us to say that. We loved it. When finished, we would help light the coal fire, which was a sawn-off 44-gallon drum placed on old demolition bricks. When the coals were right, we would bake large potatoes. If lucky—seldom, while rationing was still in force—this was served with a knob of butter and lots of salt. We would devour all of them, skins and burnt bits too.

Whilst waiting for our potatoes to bake, Dougal would tell us stories. His faithful dog roasted his tummy by the glowing coals of the fire. The stories were incredible— mostly about ghosts, goblins, strange sea creatures, fairies, witches, castles, magic rocks and dragons. He never told the same story twice. We never left our sentry box, as we called it, till our parents were heard to shout, calling us home. We often pretended not to hear but Dougal was insistent about obeying our parents.

One evening in 1950 after our safety light duties, I noticed Dougal's jacket hanging on a piece of old wire by the entrance. It had no sleeves and lots of small, strange pockets stitched on the outside—maybe twenty or so. Each pocket had a small flap fastened by a button similar to our shirts. I asked about the jacket, and he told me it was his 'seed jacket'.

Apparently in the First World War, Dougal spent many years in the trenches of Europe. Although he was never injured—unlike many of his friends—it left him with severe

PTSD. The name did not exist then, he just called it 'shell shock'. As a result, he had found it very, very difficult to sleep.

'That is a gift if you are a nightwatchman,' he told us. He went on to say that during the daylight hours he would spend all his time collecting seeds around London's parks and gardens. That's what his jacket was for. He would then take them home and propagate them. In the evening he would attend to his nightwatch duties.

I was intrigued, wondering why he was doing this. He explained that the war had not only killed people but all of creation—including the trees. They needed our help to repropagate and refill our parklands and recreational areas. 'They need us more than ever, especially the endangered ones,' Dougal said. 'They can't do it alone. We must help them. We need them and they need us. I must help them.'

That evening I returned home early and went to bed. Dougal's words were swimming in my mind. In the morning I looked out of the window. Our sentry hut, Dougal's canvas nightwatch home, had disappeared. Later that day a new hut arrived, along with a different nightwatchman. He was not a welcoming chap, and he had a little unfriendly dog that barked and snapped at anything that moved. Our young team of nightwatch cadets had to be disbanded. One of our greatest loves and proudest duties simply disappeared. We had no idea of what happened to Dougal or his dog. We missed them both—especially the stories and hot baked potato feasts.

Let's now jump into our TARDIS and zip forward to the late 1980s. I'd moved to Australia but was on a return visit with my wife to the old country. My old Georgian house in Chiswick had withstood the ravishes of time. However, my old playground, the bomb site, sported a new row of semi-detached dwellings with mock country-house features. Architecturally they seemed very inappropriate.

I took time to visit Kew Gardens. It was only a stone's throw from where I was born yet I'd never spent time there. It was magnificent—the incredible glasshouses, the complex embedded shrubberies, the wonderful array of colour and the aroma of different flora all dripped like jewels from heaven. A sun-filled day.

As Rosemary and I sat in the shade of a huge oak tree I noticed a small delicate shrub out of the corner of my eye. It was saturated with little blue buds, some in flower and swarming with honeybees. Because of my passion for bees, I ventured over. On the metal plaque was inscribed: *The Brownski Crying Maiden.*

My mind and heart raced back to the late 40s. The memory was so powerful that my taste buds were filled with baked potatoes dripping in butter. The voice of Dougal seemed to drift softly from the leaves of the shrub, the images of the goblins, fairies and dragons filled my inner vision. Could this shrub be somehow related to my hero of the bomb site?

That afternoon I visited the information archives at Kew Gardens. My excitement was quickly subdued because the details did not take me very far, apart from establishing the genus and variety. Most of the information was written in unpronounceable Latin.

But from there I spent a few days in London hopping from one tube station to another, visiting all kinds of dusty archival places and trailing down dismal corridors filled with documents tied with string and ribbon-tape. This was the age when the microfiche was deemed high tech and most of these documents had not yet been transferred to that format. Don't even dream about a photocopier.

After filling out reams of forms and sitting at dozens of desks on un-padded chairs and straining my eyes with little more assistance than a 40-watt incandescent lamp, Dougal's story started to emerge.

That cold winter evening in 1950 when we were all asleep, he was snatched by the police under the direction of the Home Office. He was subject to an investigation related to spying and espionage in the Second World War. Months of enquiry ticked by. However, he was eventually found innocent and released. The charge was related to a false witness and a mistaken identity. He received a note of apology from the Home Secretary but no compensation.

Over time he returned to his passion for botany. He was so passionate and prolific about seed-collecting and propagation that his fame spread among the more professional botanists. It was not long before he was inducted into the Endangered Tree Research Program at Oxford. There he was allegedly introduced to CS Lewis and become a part of the Inklings fraternity.

At Oxford he was able to hunt down a very rare tree which had not been seen since the outbreak of the First World

War: *The Crying Maiden*. It was thought that these trees were so highly sensitive to human pain and suffering they would wither and die if exposed to it for long periods of time. Two world wars were said to have been enough to send it to its final grave.

However, Dougal was a very persistent man. After much study and research he was able to find just one seed on a crag of a rock-strewn mountain in northern Wales. He germinated that seed and, over time, it started to grow. But so very slowly. Eventually, it grew to a stature where it was able to be transplanted in Kew Gardens. The tree survived and its seeds were collected. Now thousands on thousands of these trees grace the world and, in honour of Dougal, the new name they bear is the *Brownski Crying Maiden.*

The story does not end there. Dougal was awarded the Nobel Prize for Botany. I was still in a little doubt about the sketchy information I had. I needed more proof. Finally, I could rest easy. I obtained a photograph of all the Nobel Prize winners each year. In 1956 there on the stage were the recipients, everyone dressed in the evening formal wear or professorial academic gowns. However, one was not attired so. One man was dressed in a shabby jacket with twenty small pockets stitched to it. We salute you, Dougal.

Dougal was transported to another world on 22 January 1967. He landed in a place where there is no more pain and suffering, where the Crying Maiden Tree is in perpetual fruit and everlasting flower, and where its leaves are given for the healing of the nations.

Papa's Journey

JUDY ROGERS

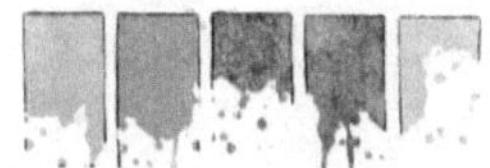

The funny thing about going on a journey is that you usually tend to gather others along the way.

Papa's journey involved all of us—

Mama, Alexander and me.

Every step Papa took us led to another discovery—

Then another—

And yet another.

Every corner, every crossroad led to the same question.

What if Papa hadn't been forced to carry the cross?

And every time the answer was the same.

All our lives—
mine
and yours
would have been different
—so very, very different.

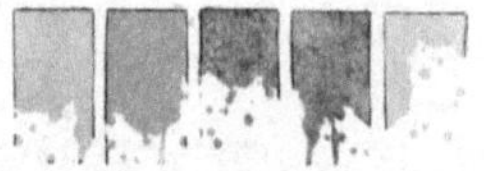

$\mathcal{P}$apa rubbed his right shoulder—yet again. His eyes glazed over.

I signalled to Alexander and together we slipped outside to tend the animals. Alexander sighed as he heaved the sheep-gate open. 'It's going to be another one of those long, silent evenings.'

Alexander was fifteen when we started this journey, and although younger than me by nearly two years, he was just as tall. Many people took us for twins—not identical twins, though. My hair is brown like Mama's. Alexander has inherited Papa's dark hair and heavy build. We've always been very close. We can share our deepest feelings and thoughts and know our secrets are safe with each other.

That evening started out the same as many of recent times—Papa's silent mood, Mama's worried eyes and animals that needed tending. The sweet smell of hay greeted us as we set to work. 'I'm really worried, Rufus.' Alexander stopped pitching hay into the pen. 'Papa hasn't been the same since we got home from celebrating Passover.'

'I know. Mama says he'll be fine, but I can see the worried look in her eyes.'

'What can we do?'

'Nothing.'

'Nothing? Come on, Rufus. There must be something! Maybe we could talk to Uncle Jacob.'

'Mama's already been to see Uncle Jacob and Uncle Benjamin.'

'Well, I guess we just have to pray and wait till Papa's ready to talk.'

I shook my head. 'Pray? Sure. You go ahead, Alexander. I wonder sometimes if God actually hears us.'

A shadow crossed the door of the barn. I swung around in horror. 'Papa! ... I didn't mean that... I didn't know you were there... I mean...'

I felt papa's strong hand on my shoulder. 'It's okay, son. It's okay to question things if you look for your answers in the right places.'

I looked into my father's brown eyes and saw a clarity there I hadn't seen in weeks. He squeezed my shoulder and smiled. 'Finish up in here, boys. Then come inside. There is something I need to discuss with you.'

Papa turned and strode out of the barn.

'Wow,' breathed Alexander. 'Did you see that? Papa smiled. He hasn't smiled since we were in Jerusalem for Passover.'

I was too stunned to answer.

Alexander and I entered the small alcove and each sat on an embroidered cushion. Mama had made them—a blue one for me and a green one for Alexander. I traced my finger around the neat outline of white sheep that had been lovingly stitched around the edge of my cushion. My cushion was part of my life. Even at seventeen, I could not think of sitting anywhere else.

I had no idea what Papa wanted to discuss, and frankly, I was rather alarmed. He had barely spoken for weeks. Papa didn't seem to notice our entrance but sat staring once more into the distance. Then he sighed and looked us each in the eye—first, Mama then me, then Alexander. 'You know,' he began. 'I have been doing a lot of thinking. So much has happened... So much has happened.' His voice trailed off.

Alexander gripped my arm.

Papa shook his head, took a deep breath and let it out very slowly. 'What if I hadn't been on the road at that very minute? What if I had started out five minutes earlier or five minutes later? What if I had walked a little faster or slower? What if we had been staying on the other side of Jerusalem or if a whim had taken me to go in at another gate? What if the centurion's eye had not chanced to alight on me in the crowd, or if he had picked out somebody else to carry the cross?'

'Ahh… the cross... the cross.' Mama sounded so tired. 'Simon, people are being crucified every day. Why is this one so different?'

'Miriam... I looked into his eyes.' Papa stared at the ceiling, and for an instant, I thought he was going to retreat back to wherever he had been going for the last few weeks.

'I looked into his eyes... They were so... so pure.' Papa's voice broke. 'And... he thanked me. He thanked me and blessed me for helping him carry his cross.'

'Oh, Simon!' Mama crossed the room and placed her hands on Papa's strong, broad shoulders. I had never noticed how tiny Mama's hands were—or maybe it was just that Papa's shoulders were so broad. Mama's hands barely seemed to make an indent as she massaged his shoulders. Yet, he leaned into her and closed his eyes.

A pained expression crossed his face. 'I stayed, you know. I stayed and watched them crucify him.'

I gasped and could feel Alexander tense beside me.

'You know they gambled for his clothes... at the foot of his cross... while he was gasping for breath... they were gambling for his clothes.' Papa cleared his throat. His voice rasped. 'He died before they came to break his legs. They pierced his side with a spear to make sure he was dead. His blood had already congealed. Blood and water gushed out.'

'Simon, please! The boys!'

'They are no longer boys, Miriam.' Papa squeezed Mama's hand and looked into my eyes. 'They are almost grown men—old enough to hear and question their faith.'

My ears burned. I dared not move.

'Do you know what he said as they nailed him to the cross?'

Mama was weeping now, and neither Alexander nor I were able to speak.

Papa's voice was barely a whisper. 'He said, "Father, forgive them. They know not what they do." He... interceded for... their forgiveness...' Papa broke down and wept.

I stared dumfounded into my brother's eyes. We had never seen Papa weep. It was too much. I grabbed Alexander's arm and we rose from the floor.

'Don't go... I need to finish.'

'Simon.' Mama's voice broke. 'We can speak about it another time.'

'No... No... I need to finish now. I am sorry, my dear.' Papa swallowed. 'I need to finish.'

Alexander and I slipped back onto our cushions. I didn't know where to look and I could feel Alexander's discomfort equalled mine.

Papa's voice regained its strength. 'Do you remember the sudden darkness that dropped over the earth that day?' Papa surveyed each of us as we stared transfixed. 'That happened while he hung on the cross... when he cried, "My God, My God. Why have you forsaken me?" It was almost as if God couldn't look at him hanging there.'

'What?' Alexander and I stared at each other.

'Yes. The world went black for three hours.' Papa stared into space and cleared his throat. 'Then he died... and do you know what happened at that precise moment?'

Papa continued without waiting for an answer.

'The veil in the temple was torn in two... from top to bottom! From top to bottom! No man could have possibly done that.' Papa leant forward and whispered. 'So, who do you think did it?'

He didn't seem to want an answer. To tell the truth, I doubt I would have been able to answer. My throat was constricted, my body frozen.

'I have been doing a lot of thinking.' Papa's voice began to waver again. I was still not game to look at him for fear of seeing the pain in his eyes. Papa cleared his throat. 'I think his cry was pointing us all to Psalm 22. Rufus, fetch the Scriptures, please.'

I glanced at Mama. She nodded slightly, so I rose to collect the scrolls. There were not many people with copies of the writings, but Papa had transcribed the scripts with his strong, neat handwriting when he was in Jerusalem many years ago. I passed the scroll to Papa. Somehow, they looked like they belonged in his big sturdy hands.

'Read, please, Alexander.'

Alexander's eyes nearly popped out of his head. 'Me? But Papa, you always read the scriptures.'

'Not today, Son. Read from here, please.'

Alexander swallowed and began to read.

> *For dogs have surrounded me;*
> *The congregation of the wicked has enclosed me.*
> *They pierce my hands and my feet;*
> *I can count my bones.*
> *They look and stare at me.*
> *They divide my garments among them and for my clothing*
> *they cast lots.*

Alexander looked at me. I'm sure our puzzled expressions mirrored one another.

'Well done, son. Now think about what I told you of the crucifixion I witnessed.'

Alexander frowned. 'They pierced his hands and his feet?'

'Yes. Yes. What else?... Rufus?'

'You said they gambled for his clothes.'

'Yes! Yes! Exactly... just as David foretold... *"They divide my garments among them and for my clothes they cast lots."* See! It's written right here! Now Rufus, your turn to read.'

Papa was beginning to get rather excited, and I was beginning to get more than a little scared, but I read the verse Papa pointed to.

He guards all his bones. Not one of them is broken.

Papa's eyes were wild with excitement. 'Don't you see? They didn't break his legs like they did to the others. David prophesied this too! It's all there... in the Scripture!'

I could sense Mama's alarm. I think it was easier when Papa was in his shell staring into nothing. 'Simon, please.'

'Just one more Miriam... or maybe two.' He grinned and winked at Mama. She rolled her eyes and shook her head. Papa's eyes twinkled. 'I'm reading this one. But first, I need to tell you about the trial.'

'The trial?' Alexander's curiosity shone in his eyes.

'This man, Jesus was betrayed by one of his friends and sold for thirty pieces of silver.'

Mama gasped. 'What friend would do that?'

'Exactly... Nevertheless, it happened. Not only did it happen, but Zechariah prophesied that it would.'

If you think it best, give me my pay; but if not, keep it. So they paid me thirty pieces of silver.

'Oh, my,' gasped Mama.

Papa continued. 'Jesus was taken to be judged, but no one could agree on what he had done wrong. Finally, he was taken to Pilate who offered to set him free as the yearly prisoner exchange—but the crowd was stirred up, and that's when they decided to crucify him.' Papa's face clouded over.

'They didn't just crucify him. First, they beat him and pulled out his beard and spat on him and mocked him. They even made a crown of thorns and rammed it on his head.'

Mama gasped. I felt sick. Alexander stared at Papa as though he was a ghost.

'I'm sorry, Miriam. I need to explain everything. This is the next reading written by the prophet Isaiah.'

I gave my back to those who struck me and my cheeks to those who plucked out the beard. I did not hide my face from shame and spitting.

'How did Isaiah know that was going to happen?' Alexander was incredulous.

'Exactly,' continued Papa. 'How did he know? Except that God told him. Why did God tell him? That's the question we need to ask.'

My curiosity was thrumming. 'Didn't they crucify him with others, Papa? How do we know it was him that Isaiah was talking about?'

'Now you are thinking, son! Jesus was crucified between two thieves.'

'And?'

'And when he had died, he was placed in a grave of a rich friend.'

'And?'

'Read for yourself, Rufus. It's here.'

I stared at Papa. 'How can it be all there? Isaiah lived hundreds of years ago.'

'Read,' Papa commanded.

So I read.

> *He was oppressed and he was afflicted, yet, he opened not his mouth.*
> *He was led as a lamb to the slaughter. And they made his grave with the wicked but with the rich at his death, because he had done no violence nor was any deceit in his mouth.*

The chills that crept up and down my spine almost made me collapse. Mama began to weep again and Alexander's mouth hung like a gaping cave.

'Who was this man?' Mama whispered.

'It's your turn to read, Miriam.'

Alexander and I stared at each other. Mama never read the scrolls.

'Simon... I...'

'Miriam, please... this section here... from Isaiah again.'

Mama's hand trembled as she took the sacred scroll from Papa.

> *For a child will be born to us, a son will be given to us; and the government will rest on his shoulders; and his name will be called Wonderful Counsellor, Mighty God, Eternal Father, Prince of Peace. There will be no end to the increase of his government or of peace, on the throne of David and over his kingdom, to establish it and to uphold it with justice and righteousness from then on and forevermore. The zeal of the Lord of hosts will accomplish this.*

Mama clutched the scrolls to her chest. 'This is the one,' she whispered. 'The one the prophecies are written about! The Messiah!'

Fresh tears rolled down her cheeks. Papa's eyes were glistening. Alexander and I stared from parent to parent and then back at each other.

I fell to my knees. 'The Messiah!' Every fibre in my being quivered with excitement. Without a shadow of doubt, I believed.

'We must go to Jerusalem,' Mama whispered. 'All of us.'

Papa grinned. 'If we leave in two days, we'll be there in time for the Feast of Pentecost.'

I could almost see the plans forming in Mama's head — lists of things to pack and food to prepare. 'I'll be ready,' she whispered. A fresh gleam shone in her eyes. She swung around and embraced Papa. 'I'll be ready.'

Alexander and I grinned at each other.

Jerusalem!

After the Well

PAMELA JULIAN

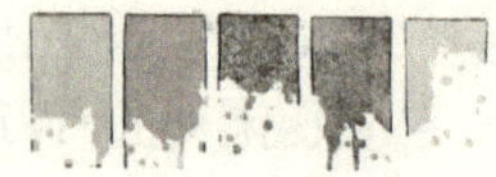

I'm no saint; well, at least, I wasn't. In fact I was about as far from sainthood as you could've got, back then.

There we were—Us who are ignored, sandwiched between two groups of Them who don't speak to us. Us and Them. It's been like that for centuries. I'm one of Us who are ignored—mind you, due to my unsaintly lifestyle, I've been ignored by a lot of Us as well as Them.

Anyway, one day I go to the well, late as usual to avoid the being ignored bit, and there he was—one of Them, sitting by the well. Surprised, I was, seeing as we're a bit out of the way here. Well, we're not really *out* of the way; in fact, we're right *in* the way, but They go out of their way to avoid Us.

So there he sat. 'Give me a drink,' he says, just like that. Gobsmacked, I was. When was the last time one of Them even spoke to one of Us—and me a woman! Anyway, we got chatting. He was easy to talk to. Fancy I even flirted with him, just a little! Funny man—said he'd give me some sort of water—he didn't even have a cup! Anyway, he kept talking about living water and fountains inside of us, and never being thirsty again. Didn't make any sense at the time.

Then he starts telling me stuff about my life! Aha, I think—a prophet! So I reckon I'll ask him a few questions about God. Been thinking about Him a lot lately—don't seem to have made too good a go of my life myself, and I'm wondering if God has any more to offer.

So, I asked him about Mount Gerizim. Always puzzled me, that. We read the books of Moses; we worship Yahweh, same as Them. We even live in Abraham's land. Yet They insist we worship in the wrong spot. *They*, of course, worship in the right spot. So I ask this bloke to explain it.

Well, blow me down if he doesn't start saying nowhere is the right spot, and we should be talking to God in spirit and in truth. Totally lost me. So I thought I'd bring it back onto safe ground—show him that I knew about the Messiah. And, wouldn't you know it? 'I am the Messiah,' he says.

Kinda made sense, I guess, him knowing all about me and all.

Just then a pack of his hairy mates arrive with lunch. A whole lot of Them. And me the only woman. You could see they thought it pretty odd that we'd been chatting, but none of them said anything, so I shot through.

On the way back into town, I got to thinking—if what he said was true, maybe God might have that something I was looking for—I've tried *everything* else. So I told the whole story to everyone I met—he said, and then I said, then he said. And that he told me my life's story. They all listened—

not often I get to be the centre of attention like that; it was kind of nice. Anyway, they all think I'm onto something too. 'Where'd you say he was?' they asked. Seems I'm not the only one thinking about God lately.

So off we went, back to the well. I was pretty excited by then. We got there just as they were finishing their sangers—all except the Messiah—maybe he could do the same thing with food as with that water of his, you know, so you'd never get hungry again!

The mayor and the others all fire questions at him, and he takes it pretty calmly. You can see they just can't get enough of what he has to say. So the mayor asks him to stay awhile.

'Psst!' I says. 'He's in a hurry. Why else would he have taken this shortcut?'

But it seems he's not in that much of a hurry after all, and he stays. We all sit around having a pretty good chinwag for a couple of days. Then, 'We're off,' he says, and they pick up their stuff and go.

Well, didn't they leave us with plenty to talk about? Most excitement in our little patch in a long while. The others all said to me, 'We only thought he was the Messiah because you were so convincing, but now we've met him, we *know*.'

I never got to be the centre of attention like that again, but my neighbours are really good to me now. Changed my life somehow…

The Dream

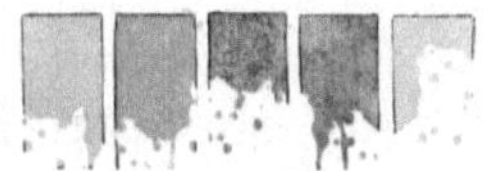

EMELY WEILER

*O*ne cold morning, in the village of Iciville, two orphans were lying huddled together under a towering pine tree. The tree protected them from the hard snow. The children had no home and barely any clothes. The girl's name was Ezra and the boy's name was Julius. They were nine and five years of age and that was a horrible time of life to be out on the streets all alone.

For the last two years, they had been by themselves and poor Ezra had been taking care of Julius. It was harsh and cold in this weather but they were determined to survive. Each morning Ezra went to the market and sang to earn the little money they needed to live. With that, she bought food and sometimes she was able to afford some extra clothes for them to wear when it was cold.

At night, they prayed that they would be warm and loved by loving parents who had enough money to raise them properly.

One day, when Ezra was singing, a handsome man heard her and gave her twenty dollars. She was wearing rags and he saw that she was homeless. 'You don't deserve to be on the street. You have the most beautiful voice that I have ever heard,' he whispered in a very warm and gentle voice. With that, he hurried away only to return with the fluffiest blanket Ezra had ever seen. In awe she stared at him, her eyes brimming with happy tears. Suddenly, she leapt forward and gave the gentleman a bear hug.

He smiled at her.

'Thank you, sir!' she gasped and, not knowing what she was doing, she rushed to show it to her little brother. When he saw it, he looked astounded.

'Did you rob a bank?' he asked as she covered him in the blanket.

'Nope,' she said. 'A nice gentleman gave it to me. Let's try to go to sleep now.'

After ten minutes of lying under the blanket Ezra and her brother were fast asleep. And for the first time this winter they were really warm.

In her excitement, Ezra forgot to take her money with her. The young man was left standing there, wondering if he should take the money to her. He decided to do so, pocketed the money and got out his wallet. With some left-over money, he bought food and cakes so the three of them could have their very own feast. After he had bought all these delicacies, he looked around to find where the little girl had disappeared.

It was very easy following the small footprints of the girl. After a while he found a big pine tree. Underneath it was a big red velvet blanket with two little lumps underneath it. For a moment he was puzzled. Then he put two and two together and figured that the other lump must be some sibling. Gently he tapped on the mound and a second later a tousled little head poked out of the blanket. The boy quickly woke his sister and, when she saw the man, she whispered something into the boy's ear. As soon as she did, his little eyes lit up with awe.

'Are you the nice man who gave Ezra this blanket?' he asked curiously.

'Yes, I am indeed,' the man laughed. 'Did your sister already tell you about me?'

'Yes, she did!' he babbled. 'You are the nicest person I ever met!'

The gentleman replied, 'I'm not even finished yet.' From behind his back, he pulled out the biggest box they had ever seen.

'Wow!' gasped Julius, 'What is that?'

His sister shared his amazement, 'I know!' she cried, 'It's a cake box!'

'It is indeed,' announced the gent, 'But how did you know that?'

Ezra told him that she had seen people buying cake and taking them home in the same boxes.

'Can you open it?' said little Julius, shivering with anticipation.

The young man passed him the box. 'No,' he said. 'You should open it.'

Julius gently took the box. Ezra leaned in as he opened it. When she saw the cake, she promptly fainted. When she revived, she was tongue-tied. They had never seen so many yummy goodies in their life. Julius grabbed at something to see if it was real. It was.

A few minutes later, they were sitting around the box each with a little cake in their hand. They each ate two pieces and the cake melted in their mouths. In the end everybody claimed it to be the best cake they had ever had and would have for their whole life. And that was true.

The man stayed until dusk and then made his way back home. Just before he disappeared from their sight, he stopped abruptly and said, 'What a forgetful person I am! I haven't given you your money back! You forgot it when I gave you the blanket!'

'Oh, thank you so much!' Ezra replied with gratitude, 'I did forget it!'

The next day Ezra and Julius woke up feeling magnificent. The taste of cake was still lingering in their mouths. It was the best night's sleep they had ever had while living in the streets because the quilt kept them warm and toasty.

Before breakfast, Ezra went to the market to sing again. She wanted to buy some shoes for Julius because he was slowly getting blue feet. Winter was nearly over (which was a relief) because then they wouldn't waste their money on clothes. She sang ever so beautifully and earned $25 and 95 cents. For breakfast she bought bread, butter and tea.

They ate it under the blanket, feeling so immensely carefree. They had a very fine day, walking around the town and peering into all of the different shops that lined the narrow streets. For dinner, they had a pie a lady in a shop had given them. It was one of the finest days they had had for a long time. They had a fabulous night's sleep.

The next day the young gentleman appeared at their blanket again, wishing them a good morning. They invited him to lunch. Lunch consisted of an apple, some bread with cheese and water. For dessert they had a cake that Ezra had bought from the money she had worked for.

They talked and Ezra wanted to pay back the gent because the cake was very expensive. He refused. Then the gentleman finally introduced himself. 'My name is John Sinnette,' he announced proudly.

'Wow!' said Julius, 'That's a very posh name. Are you rich?'

John laughed. 'You could say that,' he agreed. 'I live in a mansion not far away from here.'

Julius stared at him in shock and admiration, 'A mansion? Really?'

Ezra was also shocked. 'Do you have any children?' she asked.

'No, I don't,' he said rather sadly. 'My wife can't have any babies.'

Julius frowned. 'Couldn't we be your children?' he asked, wide-eyed.

John stared and then he fell down in a heap. They wondered what was wrong with him so they waited for him to straighten up again. When he did, tears were shining in his eyes.

'What's wrong?' asked Ezra, wiping the tears off his smiling face.

'Well,' he said thoughtfully, 'I'll ask my wife and maybe she'll say yes.'

'Oh really?' asked Julius, his eyes shining in pleasure. 'That would be wonderful!'

They had a snowball fight with him and, in the end, their faces were glowing with exhaustion. For dinner, they went to a diner that was only a few minutes away from their tree. John bought them some soup with noodles bobbing around in it.

'What are those?' Julius asked, looking at the noodles in suspicion.

'Those are noodles,' explained John.' They are yummy.'

Still eyeing them with suspicion Julius took a string and popped it in his mouth. His eyes widened in surprise. It tasted delicious. He took another one and after thirty seconds all the noodles had disappeared from his bowl. Then he picked up the bowl and poured the lukewarm broth down his throat.

He rubbed his stomach. 'I feel all warm in my tummy now,' he said, creasing his eyebrows.

John was grinning in a most funny way. His eyes were twinkling and the edges of his mouth were twitching furiously. Seconds later, he collapsed into a fit of giggles. They were so infectious that Ezra and Julius were doubled over seconds later, almost screaming with laughter.

When they finally calmed down, Ezra had her head in her soup bowl. She pulled it out and the soup splashed onto the floor, soaking her in the process. When Julius and John saw her covered in soup, they burst out laughing all over again.

John went to the bathroom to wash off some cake that was stuck in his hair like gum. He returned looking rosy-cheeked and immensely handsome. In his hand he held a plate and on it were eclairs, donuts, a cake and six little cakes.

Ezra and Julius groaned in unison. 'How on earth are we going to eat all that?' Ezra asked, wondering how much John was paying for this absolutely expensive meal.

'Oh, I should have thought of that,' sighed John. 'You won't be able to eat this. Maybe I will give it back to the diner.'

Ezra and Julius looked at him in indignation. 'But...' Ezra stammered, 'But can't we take it to our tree?' She looked hurt.

'Of course, you can,' John said, 'I was only joking.'

Julius sighed in utmost relief. 'Thank heavens,' he said. 'I thought you really meant that.'

John looked sorry. 'I didn't mean to scare you. I thought you might understand a little joke.'

'Don't be sorry.' Ezra soothed him, 'We just haven't ever had anyone joke like that before, so we couldn't understand it.'

This comment did exactly the opposite of cheering John up. He decided that he definitely needed to persuade his wife to adopt these kids. When he was gone, Ezra and Julius prayed and prayed for their most-wished-for wish to come true.

The next morning it was snowing slightly and Ezra was woken up by a snowflake that had gone up her nose. She sneezed loudly and woke up Julius.

'What is that?' he asked, as a clump of snow landed on his head. When he sat up, he saw the white falling snow all around him. 'Oh, snow!' he cried happily, and stuck out his tongue to catch some flakes. As usual, John appeared shortly after Ezra had started singing. Singing hymns about Jesus, she earned $68!

When John saw it, he raised his eyebrows, impressed. 'You made half a fortune today, darling.'

With the money they bought pancakes at the café nearby. Full of breakfast they made their way back to the tree to talk. John said that he had talked to his wife about adopting them. They listened eagerly as John related their conversation. 'My wife said yes, but you don't have any bedrooms yet,' he explained carefully.

'We don't mind sleeping on the floor for a few days! Do we, Ezra?' asked Julius excitedly. He wanted to belong to a family as soon as possible. 'If it would be possible.'

'I'll think about it,' agreed John.

'Yay!' shouted Julius joyfully. 'Thanks, John!'

They spent the day playing cards and snowball-fighting. Happy was the wrong word for them. They were ecstatic! They laughed, shouted and had the best of fun all the way until dinner-time. Later that night, they went to a diner and Julius wasn't wary of the food anymore, for he had become used to the weird, unknown, yummy foods that John seemed to know. Ezra found that pizza was now her most favourite food of all the new dishes she had tried in the last week. After dinner they made their way to a parking lot behind the diner.

'Why are we going here?' asked Ezra. 'Didn't you say you lived in a mansion? I don't see any mansion here.'

Without explaining, John led them to a long car. For Julius it didn't take long to realise. He gaped at John. 'This is your car?' he asked, fascinated, but not completely surprised. He felt that anything could happen with this man.

After a short drive they went through a hedge cave and John announced, 'This is where my property starts.' They continued in it for a while until they came out in a field where some cows grazed. All of them had golden bells around their necks that dangled prettily when they looked up to see who was driving past. One of them mooed loudly and scared Julius because he had never heard one before. Ezra soothed him and told him that they were very safely protected in the car. They drove over gravel and five minutes later they saw five turrets on the horizon. 'Wow!' breathed Ezra, 'That's beautiful!'

In silence they looked at the mansion as they drew closer. 'This is my kingdom!' John said, scarcely louder than a whisper. 'You are finally adopted.'

Moral of the story:
Believe in what you want and you could make it come to life and never, ever give up on your dreams.

Dimitri — the Wood Carver

TERRY GATFIELD

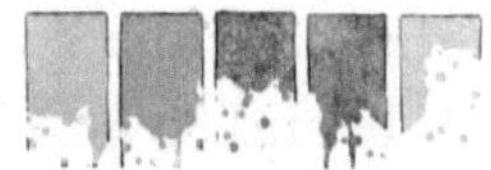

It was a damp Saturday evening in autumn, around sixish, as we slowly strolled down the Queen Street Mall towards the Story Bridge. I was with my old friend, Chris. I had not seen him in many years. Divorced by our over-busy lives, he was working at the ASX, which always remained a mystery and a black-art to me. Chris also involved himself in charity work. I, being of a more modest persuasion, ran an automobile garage. It was good to be back in his company.

Saturday nights were aways special for me as they provided the opportunity to unwind and forget about motor mechanics, spare parts, customer issues and eternal staffing problems. It was one of those precious nights usually reserved for spending time with like-minded friends. This was one of those evenings accompanied with a little social lubricant and some munchies.

As we slowly continued our journey, I suddenly found myself walking alone.

Chris had stopped at a little laneway off to the right. I retreated and saw him in the shadows standing alongside an old beggar. Not unusual. But the beggar was somewhat different. He sat on an old wooden crate, with a chocolate-coloured Labrador munching on a Jurassic-park-sized bone. The dog's tail was wagging with a regular beat as if he was keeping time for an invisible orchestra. The old man wore old winter warm clothes, but was not shabbily attired; his hair was longish but not untidy and covered by a dark beanie. By his side was a very large thermos flask. It was one of those old-fashioned types made of stainless steel and with chipped enamel paint. The top was off, and steam was emerging from its neck. For a brief moment it flashed into my mind that I was witnessing the opening scene of Shakespeare's *Macbeth*, minus the witches. Just then Chris opened his wallet and dispatched a $50 note into the old man's hand, gave a wink and without a word turned on his heel.

'What was that all about?' I asked after we were out of earshot.

'Oh, that was Dimitri, have you not met him before? He is something of an icon in my life. Let's find somewhere to sit, have a glass of wine and get some hot wedges and sour cream. I'm peckish. I'll tell you the story.'

That was such a joyful evening as Chris shared the story of Dimitri and, as far as I can recall, it went something like this.

Dimitri was Russian, as you would have gathered with a name like that. He was born in Australia about two years after his parents had emigrated during the Second

World War. He was their only child and much loved. His father encouraged Dimitri in music, and he became a highly accomplished violinist. In due season he had won many awards and accolades and was offered a scholarship to further his ambitions and career in music. Some thought he was a prodigy as he was able to play all of Bach's sonatas and partitas without reading written scores. Alas, at age 15 he developed an ear infection which was left untreated as his parents could not afford specialist treatment and expensive medications. In a short period of time his hearing had deteriorated to the extent that he had to abandon his beloved violin and his future music career.

However, his love and passion for the beauty of the violin did not diminish. He turned his heart and soul to repairing, refurbishing and servicing the instrument. Mainly self-taught, Dimitri became highly skilled in this profession, but it was not easy. Sycamore, German maple, Romanian gliga, Carpathian spruce, Californian redwood, ebony and huon pine were not easily sourced, and suppliers were few and far between. Also, his craftsmanship was impeded by the Australian extreme seasons and weather patterns. Sub-zero to high 40's and from zero to 90% humidity were unwelcome companions. Yet, a new and even more exciting door was to open for him.

The overseas supplies of exotic timbers were usually spliced very thin and parcelled in a way to preserve their integrity. Thus, the highly priced thin veneers were often sandwiched between larger pieces of similar materials to prevent premature drying. That wood was only packaging and of much lesser quality.

In a quiet moment Dimitri decided to fashion one of the packaging pieces with his pocketknife. He made a little mouse, and soon after he created a small squirrel and then a series of large ants. The wonders of creation had entered his soul.

As months moved by his passion for wood carving increased. His menagerie extended and soon he received orders from people all over Australia. Within a year or so demand had increased so he transferred his work on violins to creating animals, birds, insects—anything that would scratch, creep, walk or fly. His raw materials were now the cedars, oaks, pines, ash, myrtle, jarrahs, and gums. Dimitri explored oils and finishes and before long he was sourcing resins and natural pigments from Romania, Brazil, Egypt and Peru and reviving timber finishes long lost in annals of time.

Dimitri understood the language of his timbers. He would often say, 'Listen carefully to their music and respect their texture and rhythms.' On one occasion he found a large piece of seasoned silky oak, not the heart of the tree with nicely ordered grain, but one of the outer planks from the thick, rough bark of the tree. Normally this would have become fuel for the Sunday afternoon BBQ. It was gnarly, thick, calloused, resinous and had a large uneven weathered gap as large as a fist in the middle along with a host of small cracks. He laid it on a bench for months till he heard its voice. In the weeks that followed it was rebirthed into a living landscape of hills, valleys, creeks, fissures, culverts and ravines. He of course included a number of his small native animals in the narrative. Some of the timber was left rough to the touch and some polished as smooth as glass. It was saturated in colours, from a translucent opaque red to deep greens and purples. It was purchased at an exhibition for a private collection. He regretted that sale and mourned for many a season. In hindsight he felt that the trees were God's gift for all of humanity and not just for the rich to enjoy.

Around this time Dimitri's father had died; his mother having passed away some years previously. The modest family home was sold, and he purchased an old, small factory in a disused industrial estate. Half of the factory premises he converted into a small, comfortable flat while the other half was dedicated to his dream of creating a place to provide a fellowship of wood carvers and like-minded aficionados.

The word got around and in the ensuing months a colony of interested wood carvers came together. They were generally rough and inexperienced, but he guided them gently. 'The first rule to select the piece of timber,' he informed them, 'is the necessity to hear its soul through its voice. This is its music and found through sensing it with hands, through smelling and listening to the orchestra of its heritage, the woodland and the coppice. The form, grain and texture will always yield its secrets and will guide you, the craftsman, on the right journey. Nothing should be rushed. Harmony must prevail. Transcendence is essential.'

As the fraternity matured, divergence emerged. Some items created were of table top interest both abstract and otherwise;

some became items of art to parade on the wall. Others took a utilitarian function. Imagination was without boundaries.

Dimitri commenced weekly class for his emerging masters. A local school principal heard of his skills and invited Dimitri to talk to a class of young students. It was a mega-hit. He brought with him a collection of small wood carved animals and fish. The children gravitated to them, gave them voices and names and danced around the room with the wood carvings, talking to each other. It gave him an opportunity to talk of the wonders of the various types of timbers and how we can use them in a richer way in our society—as indeed they were one of the very rare renewable resources. Soon Dimitri's fame spread around the schools, and he became in great demand—yes, and he also brought with him his faithful chocolate Labrador.

Dimitri is still alive and active, and his presence is still found in Brisbane—it certainly is now with me. Oh, you may be wondering why he was sitting down in the cold dark alleyway that Saturday night?

Chris explained: 'Dimitri has a passion to make himself available to the max and to all people. That dark alley is like a place for confession for some. For others, an opening to get counsel and for many just a place to share their joys, sorrows and aspirations. Dimitri would often stay there for many a day and night.'

Chris, my friend, was one of his supporters.

Martha's Secret
JUDY ROGERS

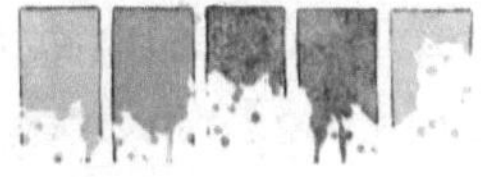

I'll never forget His eyes!
—How glorious—
—full of fire—
Yet so peaceful.
They stared straight into me—
Through me.
Into the depths of my soul—
Into my spirit.

THE SECRET

'Tell me your biggest secret.' Simon's eyes sparkled with mischief.

'What?'

'Your biggest secret,' Simon repeated. 'I know you have a secret. Something has changed in you.'

I stared past him. 'Nothing's changed.'

'Martha, we've known each other for eleven years—since we were babies. Come on... what is it?'

I really liked Simon. Fortunately, we were still young enough for our friendship to be innocent, but sometimes—sometimes, I dream of his big brown eyes and imagine being lost in the depths of their softness. *I wonder what it would be like to have him look at me the way Joshua looks at my cousin?*

'What are you smiling about, Martha? Must be some secret.'

I gasped and shook my head. *Dare I tell him?* I spun around and looked him straight in the eye. 'Okay. You're right. Something did happen.'

'I knew it!' Simon lay back on the grass with his hands behind his head. I could see the smug look on his face. 'Well, come on,' he teased.

I took a deep breath and held it for a few seconds. 'I died last year.'

'Oh, funny girl.' Simon rolled onto his stomach. 'You died. Yeah, sure, Martha.'

'It was glorious, Simon! The colours! The music! Sometimes I lie awake at night and try to recapture it all—but I can't.'

I glanced at Simon. His throat was jumping up and down. His mouth hung open. I turned away. 'Well, you did ask.'

There was no answer. 'Simon, I'm telling the truth.' I jumped to my feet. 'But if you don't believe me—fine!' I stomped off with the biggest show I could muster.

'Hey, Martha, wait up.' Simon's breath was in my ear. He grabbed my arm. 'I'm sorry. That wasn't the sort of secret I was expecting.'

The rage that had been threatening to choke me subsided. I never had been able to stay angry with Simon for long. 'Yeah, well, I guess it is kind of hard to believe.' I spun around to face him. 'But it really did happen, Simon. I really did die.'

'How? I mean—you died? Died... like dead?'

'Of course I "died like dead"—is there any other sort of "died"?'

This was the first time I'd spoken to anyone outside my own family about that day. I was regretting my decision, but I figured I'd come too far to opt out now. Besides this was Simon. We'd shared secrets since I could remember. I took a deep breath. 'Remember last year when I got sick?'

'That was a bad time.' Simon stared into the distance. 'Lots of people got sick.'

I could see him close his eyes and swallow. 'That's when Jared...' Simon stopped walking. He spun around to face me. Pain contorted his face. I wished I could say something—do something to help. He turned away. 'You know, Martha,' Simon spoke to the air. 'Sometimes I wish Jared had died instead of...' His voice trailed off for a moment. 'Martha, he can't do anything—can't feed himself, can't dress himself... can't even...'

My throat tightened. Jared had been like a big brother to me as well as to Simon. Our families shared meals on top of each other's houses in the summer months. We even built our sukkot next to each other.

'Mama's so weary these days and I don't know what to do. Jared's too heavy for me to lift. I hate to see Mama struggling and Papa works long hours and doesn't get home 'til late. If it wasn't for your family, we wouldn't be able to manage anything.' Simon dragged his hand across his eyes leaving a dirty smudge.

I steered him to a tree and we sat in the shade. The village became a blur as my eyes filled with tears. Guilt washed over me. I pulled my knees up under my chin. *Why was I healed and not Jared?*

Just because mama asked Jesus to heal me. It was as simple as that. Anyhow Jared wasn't very sick when Jesus passed through Bethphage.

'I'm sorry, Martha. Tell me what happened.'

I stared into the distance. The spring sunlight danced on the stones of the village wall. The mid-day haze played on the rooftops.

'Sometimes I lie awake at night and try to remember the warmth that spread throughout my body—the tingling tenderness and power... It started from my hands. Then I heard the voice... reverberating throughout my spirit. It was outside me and inside me at the same time. *"Little girl, wake up."'* I swung to face Simon. 'Try as I might, I can't recapture it.'

'It really happened—like that?'

I nodded. 'I know I heard it—felt it… And His eyes! I will never forget them—so glorious—full of fire—yet so peaceful. They stared straight into me—into the depths of my soul.'

Simon was silent for a while. 'Martha, you know they killed Him,' he whispered.

'Killed who?'

'Jesus. They killed Him.'

My heart lurched. 'What?'

'They killed Him.'

'Who killed Him?'

Simon scratched in the dirt. 'The Scribes and Pharisees.'

'Why?'

'Papa says they were jealous of Him because He taught with authority and pointed out ways they were not keeping God's message.'

New tears streamed down my face. 'I don't believe it!'

'It's true. It happened at Passover.'

I could feel my chest convulsing as I gasped for breath.

'I'm sorry, Martha. I thought you knew. But they say He came back to life.'

I lifted my head and stared at Simon, aware of the anguish on my face. 'What?'

'They say He came back to life.'

'Where is He now?'

'I'm not sure, but heaps of people say they've seen Him.'

'Simon, we have to find Him. We have to ask Him to heal Jared. Don't you see? He can heal Jared!' I grabbed Simon's hand and pulled him up. 'Come on!'

'Martha, He died!'

I stepped right up to Simon's face. 'So did I.'

Simon's brown skin paled. His eyes stilled. 'Come on!' He grabbed my hand and together we ran to the village.

HOPE

I burst through the door and ran straight into Papa. 'Papa! They killed Jesus!'

'Whoa!' I felt Papa's strong arms around me and I struggled against them. It was no use. Papa held me securely. I gave up struggling and fell into his chest, sobbing. He held me close. His steady heart beat soon calmed me. 'Martha,' he whispered into my hair.

'Why didn't you tell me?'

Mama and Papa exchanged strange glances. Mama sighed. 'We didn't want you to be upset.'

'You're right,' I whispered. I hugged Papa and straightened up on his lap. 'Did you know He came back to life?'

'Where did you hear that?'

'Simon told me. He said heaps of people have seen Him.'

A strange look crossed between my parents. Mama knelt down in front of me. 'Martha, I guess you really need to hear the whole story.' She glanced at Papa again. 'Jesus was betrayed by one of His followers.'

'What? Who would do that?'

'It was Judas,' Mama whispered.

'Judas?' I swallowed. 'Why?'

'Some say greed. But he couldn't bear the guilt so he... killed himself.'

'Judas? Killed himself?' I fell back against Papa's chest. Judas was a friend of my Uncle James.

A new determination rose within me. 'Papa, we have to find Him. We have to find Jesus!'

Papa frowned. 'We already thanked Him for healing you, Martha.'

'You don't understand, Papa.' My voice squeaked. 'He can heal Jared!'

'Martha,' Mama's eyes were tender. 'Jared can't walk or talk.'

'Yes, Mama... and I was dead!'

Papa stood up so fast I almost tumbled off his lap. 'I'll be right back.' His voice was hoarse and I could see his eyes shining as he hurried out the door.

Mama was grinning from ear to ear. 'Martha, you're amazing!' She swooped down and hugged me tight. 'Come, I promised Joanna I'd make dinner for her family. She has given me lamb to cook. Eli's not home from work yet and Jared's having a bad day.' Soon the aroma of chopped herbs and spicy lamb filled the kitchen. My heart was singing. I knew Jesus would heal Jared. We just had to find Him.

'Mmm, that smells good!' Papa's big frame filled the doorway. His white teeth sparkled amongst his beard.

'What have you been up to, Josiah?' Mama pointed the wooden stirring spoon at Papa. 'Don't just stand there like a grinning donkey.' Mama crossed the room and went to Papa. His big, muscular arms encircled her. I hadn't realized how small Mama was 'til then. Her arms didn't even make it around Papa's middle.

A shadow crossed the doorway. Simon's papa, Eli—face ashen, tears streaming down his face—stumbled through the door. 'Do you really think Jared can be healed?' he whispered. I could see his jaw working hard.

'Eli, come in.' Papa led our dear friend to a stool. Eli sat heavily and rested his head in his hands. 'We know Jesus can heal Jared.' Papa rested his big hand on Eli's shoulder. 'I don't know why we didn't think of it before.'

Eli looked up. His eyes were heavy-rimmed and weary. 'We have been to all the doctors.' His voice quavered. 'They said nothing can be done... and this paralysis often happens when someone has a bad fever. Usually...' Eli swallowed. '... Children die.' He glanced up at me and closed his eyes. 'Oh, Martha, I'm so sorry.'

'Uncle Eli, don't be sorry. That's exactly why we need to take Jared to Jesus. I died and He healed me. I know He can heal Jared.'

Eli shook his head. 'They killed him,' he whispered.

'Yes.' I crouched down in front of Uncle Eli and took his rough hands in mine. 'But He came back to life.'

Uncle Eli looked into my eyes for a long time. I saw a glimmer of a twinkle, then his whole face lit up. 'You're right, Martha.'

'So, it's settled?' Papa's voice boomed through the house.

'What's settled?' Mama and I spoke together.

'Jerusalem. We're going to Jerusalem. Tomorrow.'

Mama gasped. '*Tomorrow?* Come *on*, Josiah!'

'Well, then... the day after tomorrow. We'll all be in Jerusalem for Pentecost.'

Uncle Eli stood and hugged me. He smelt of leather and polish. I loved that smell. 'Martha, thank you. Thank you.' Then he hugged Papa. Together the two men danced a little jig. It was like Purim. They were so funny together.

'We'll be over as soon as dinner is cooked. I think this is a cause for celebration.'

 JERUSALEM

'Oh my!' breathed Mama. 'I've never seen so many people!'

'Stay close,' called Eli.

I certainly didn't need to be told twice. In an instant, I felt Papa lift me into the little cart he'd borrowed for the trip. Mama held me close. 'Oh, Papa, the poor donkey. Can he pull us all?' My cry was lost in the hubbub.

Lambs bleated. Donkeys brayed. Stall holders cried out. Hagglers argued. Women called. Children played tag amongst the coloured booths. Our little donkey, however, didn't flinch. His little head just bobbed up and down as he followed Papa. Every bump in the road made me cringe—not for my sake. My heart ached for Jared who was lying in the bottom of the cart in front. The road to Jerusalem had been very bumpy and very dusty.

'I wonder how Jared is handling all the noise.' I had to yell for Mama to hear me.

'My brother's house is just around the corner. It shouldn't be as bad there.'

I nodded. It was no use trying to have a conversation amongst the clamour. The donkeys plodded on through the market place and around the corner. All of a sudden, we were in a different world. The only sound was the clip-clop of our faithful donkeys' hooves.

Mama let out an audible sigh. I felt her relax against me. 'I don't understand why anyone would choose to live here.'

'Josiah! Lidia! Martha! How good to see you!'

Mama's eyes lit up.

'Uncle James!' I jumped down from the cart before it had even stopped. Uncle James engulfed me in his big bearlike arms. I loved Uncle James.

'Well, now who is this strapping young man? Can't be Simon. Simon's just a boy.' Uncle James ruffled Simon's hair and greeted his parents. 'Run along inside, you two. Sara has dates and honey cakes.'

I grabbed Simon's hand but not before I noticed the worried looks pass between the adults as they moved towards Eli's cart.

Simon saw it too. He frowned. 'Jared hasn't had a very good trip,' he whispered. 'At least he can rest more comfortably now.'

It wasn't long before we were seated on cushions around the low table. Aunt Sara made cushions to sell at the markets. Blue ones and green ones, purple ones and red ones. I chose a purple one with little camels embroidered around the edge.

'My, this lamb dish is good, Sara! Is it another new recipe?' Mama and Sara were forever exchanging cooking tips.

'I'll give it to you in the morning.' Sara smiled. 'Right now, judging by your yawns, I think it's time for bed.'

I was glad she said that. I could hardly keep my eyes open but I didn't want to miss anything. Simon was already asleep on his papa's shoulder.

 THE CITY SQUARE 

My heart lurched. 'Papa, what's that noise?' I whispered.

I felt Papa's arm tighten around me and knew his other arm held Mama. He drew us close. A bizarre rushing sound filled the air. I glanced at Simon. His face was ashen. I wondered if I looked as scared. Papa held us tight... waiting.

Nothing happened. No storm—nothing—just a sound like a mighty wind. 'I'm not sure what it is.' Papa looked around. 'Everyone's heading to the square. Come on let's go and see.'

'Josiah? Is that wise?' Mama shrunk back against the building.

'We'll stay at the edge. Don't worry, Lidia.'

'We're coming too!' Eli grabbed Simon's hand. 'Joanna and Sara are staying with Jared.'

Simon grinned at me. His hair was still tousled, his tunic askew. I shook my head.

'What's wrong, Martha?'

'I see you had honey cakes for breakfast.'

'Oh.' Simon wiped his face with the back of his hand and licked his fingers. 'Yeah,' he grinned. 'How did you guess?'

Eli's booming laugh filled the narrow street. It was so good to hear him laugh again. We could hear the commotion long before we got to the square. My heart pounding, I gripped Papa's hand with both of mine.

Peter and the disciples were up the front—babbling away in a different language!

Papa frowned. 'They certainly don't look drunk. Anyway it's only the third hour.'

I looked up at him, puzzled. Surely he realised everyone could understand them—even the Egyptians!

Peter's voice seemed too loud to be coming from one man. It filled the whole square. *'This Jesus, God has raised from the dead...'*

My heart skipped a beat. A thousand ants crawled over my head. I clutched Papa's big hand tighter. Thousands and thousands of people jammed into the square yet Peter's voice could be heard over the top of everyone. *'Therefore, let the house of Israel know assuredly that God has made this Jesus whom you crucified both Lord and Christ.'*

A great murmur arose. 'What shall we do?' someone called.

Peter raised his arms. *'Repent and let everyone of you be baptised in the name of Jesus the Christ for the redemption of sins and you shall receive the gift of the Holy Spirit.'*

With a deafening cheer, people thronged to the pool of Siloam. I tugged at Papa's hand. 'I want to go too!'

'And me,' added Simon.

Papa, Eli and Uncle James held each other's gaze for a few seconds. Big grins broke out simultaneously. Papa scooped me up, took Mama's hand. Uncle Eli held Simon's shoulder. We joined the throng.

AT THE POOL

Amongst the jostling and pushing and calling we somehow managed to stay together. At last, it was our turn. We were just about the last ones to be baptised. Oh, I will never forget that day! It was the most glorious thing—besides being raised from the dead, of course. I felt the same warmth, the same peace, the same joy.

When I came up from the water, I grabbed Peter's hand. 'Please. Where's Jesus? We need Him.'

'What do you know of Jesus, little one?'

I was nearly crying. 'We need Him.'

'Jesus has gone to Heaven.' Peter's voice sounded like a hundred angels singing.

'But He can't have!' My voice cracked. 'We need Him! Simon's brother, Jared, got the same sickness I did. But now he can't speak or feed himself... or anything! I know Jesus can heal him. I know He can!' I didn't let go of Peter's hand.

'How do you know that?'

My tears were flowing freely, mixing with the water dripping from my hair. 'Last year I died and... Jesus healed me.'

Peter looked into my eyes. I felt like I was swimming in love. 'Where is Jared?'

'At my uncle's.' I whispered.

Uncle Eli stepped forward. 'It's true, sir. Jesus raised this little girl. My son caught the same sickness and now...' Uncle Eli's voice faltered.

Peter tipped my chin up and looked deep into my eyes. A grin broke over his face. 'Take me to your friend, little one.'

A Trader in Jerusalem
BISHOP M. LESTER DIGHTON

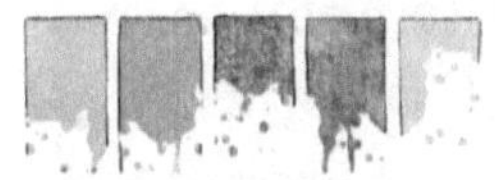

What's that, dear sir? You wish to hear this tale as well? Well, grab a tankard and sit with us so that I may share this strange tale with you.

Please allow me to introduce myself: my name is Tannock, and I am a trader in tin, and tinware. As you have heard me telling my wife, Avon, I have just returned from a journey to the fabled city of Jerusalem. I journeyed there with another trader of goods from that very destination, one by the name of Joseph, of Arimathea. He comes here to the Isles of Tarshish every so often to trade in strange and exotic goods from his native land. Of course, he takes back some of our famed local products to sell there, including tin and other precious metals. I envisioned also trading in Jerusalem with my ore and wares, so I went to see it for myself.

We loaded our goods on a vessel and sailed down past Spain and over the Great Sea to the coast of Judea, where Joseph had a caravan waiting to transport us and our chattels across the countryside. What a beautiful, and sometimes harsh, countryside it was—greatly varied in places. Along the way, I learned something of the trade language used there—a variation of the Greek, despite it being under Roman rule like we are.

I must point out that the stories told by the caravanners, and even by Joseph himself, did little to prepare me for the sight of that city. The Temple, so magnificent, so prominent in its grandeur, sat on one of its seven hills. I was struck by the spectacle. However, it is only the setting for this strange tale, and not the story itself.

While there, I did not just trade in goods, but spent time looking around this city of majesty and beauty. Joseph of Arimathea acted as my guide and companion. He translated not only the dialect of Greek they used, but a local tongue, Aramaic. It was on one of our wanderings that we came across a small group of men in the company of one Jesus of Nazareth. They were at the Temple, that glorious Temple, where they were cornered by another group of men in fine garb—Scribes and Pharisees, as I soon learned. The well-dressed men were dragging a woman along with them. They brought her before this Jesus, and said she was charged with 'Adultery'.

I had to ask Joseph what this meant. To my surprise, it was for sharing herself with another man—that's it! All of it! Well, for someone from here, where this is not a crime, but quite a normal thing, you can imagine the extent of my disbelief.

You do know, dear sir, of our Druidic rituals for Mayday? Our maidens go out into the forest after the dance of celebration where they wrap themselves around the Maypole. They lay themselves down and all the men go and share amongst them at will. As we celebrate and worship their womanhood, they take life and power from us.

All of this overseen by the 'Robin', dressed in his 'Hood' and green 'Elvin' clothing, leading the way. As you may know, sometimes we call him 'Robin Hood', a fine archer whose 'arrow' never misses. There are other occasions when we just call him the 'Green Man'. Why, my wife and I have enjoyed many of these festivals ourselves.

What a shock to discover that, over there in Jerusalem, it is a crime of major significance. Not only a serious crime, but one that is worthy of being stoned to death, if found guilty. Truly a strange idea to us, for that would be such a waste of a wonderful maiden, and her womanhood. Even the Romans don't think of it as anything bad.

However, the strangeness of my story is not about this law of the Jews. Events took an unexpected course. The maiden was released, and was told to 'go and sin no more.' Let me expand on this, for it was something out of the ordinary for everyone there.

Now I thought this Jesus of Nazareth was a judge and that the fine-garbed men were bringing the maiden to him for sentencing. Yet apparently, he wasn't a judge at all. Instead, Joseph said he was a Seer; a Prophet, a Miracle-Worker. These fine-garbed men, the Scribes and Pharisees, disliked

Jesus intensely. None of this made sense to me. I couldn't understand why you would bring someone to a Prophet for sentencing after breaking the law, instead of the official law enforcers. Yet this is what they did.

This is when things really started to get strange. Instead of announcing any judgment, He stooped down and started writing on the ground. I have no idea what He wrote, since it was in a foreign language. I wasn't sure if this was how these things were done there, just that it certainly isn't how we do it here.

Anyway, this Jesus didn't even speak to them in the manner of any judge I have ever heard of. When the men didn't get any response from Him, they asked even louder for His verdict. Then He stood up and said: 'He that is without sin, let him cast the first stone.'

I fully expected to see a flurry of rocks and stones heading her way, but—nothing! I was even prepared to start ducking the projectiles myself. Instead, everyone just stood there—as if stunned! Jesus then squatted down again and wrote once more on the ground. When the men saw him doing this, they all started to leave. I certainly have never seen any trial quite like it.

After this, Jesus asked the maiden where her accusers were, and she rightly answered that there were no one left to condemn her. This is when He told her to go home and sin no more. Can you see how strange and odd this was? Why, the woman wasn't even asked if she actually did anything, let alone something wrong. People came with loud accusations;

He wrote on the ground, in the dust near the Temple gate, and then they all left. The maiden went last of all. No one was taken out to be hung, put to the sword, stood before the archers, speared, stoned, or anything. Can you see why I think it so strange a thing to occur?

Jesus then spoke for a time with some Pharisees, while I turned to Joseph of Arimathea, and asked if he could shed any light on what had just played out in front of us.

Joseph's explanation began like this: 'In your country, do you have any marriages that do not work out?' I could only reply that this was very common everywhere. He nodded, then went on. 'I have to go back even further to give you a better understanding of what a divorce means here. When a couple are betrothed, the man furnishes a dowry to buy the bride from her parents, and even goes off to build her a house, and then she essentially becomes part of his property in that house. Not quite in the total sense—she can still work as part of the marriage, and even have a say in the running of the household.'

'This is very different from how it is done in my homeland,' I told him.

He nodded. 'Once they are wed and the marriage consummated, then it is a shameful thing for the woman to return home as a divorcee; a used woman.' As I frowned, he went on, 'In our law here, a man must give her a paper of divorcement, and place it in her hands to make it official, but that does not always happen. A woman shouldn't divorce her husband, but some still do. Without the proper paperwork, then she is still officially married, but without a husband, or a home. Naturally, a widow is exempt from this stigma, but the rest aren't. That leaves them with only a few options: return home in shame, live begging on the streets at the mercy of others, become a prostitute, or move in with another man as if married.'

'And the last is the most frequent choice?' I surmised.

Again Joseph nodded. 'We know that this woman was not caught in simply a random act of adultery, for both the man and the woman must be brought before the Priests for sentencing in these cases. She was not accused of prostitution, so we can rule that one out too. This leaves co-habitation as the most likely cause of her predicament. Normally, people caught up thus are taken before the Priests of the Temple, who make the judgment call.'

That was the moment when I became sure, beyond any doubt, that what I'd seen was not normal, even in this strange culture.

'Now, the Priests do understand that not all are guilty of wilful crimes,' Joseph continued. 'Some are innocent victims of some selfish people. However, under our law, they are still required to record the offences committed, and in a certain format. So what do they do? The answer lies in the scrolls of the Prophet Jeremiah. When addressing the harlotry of the nation of Israel—the name of our land centuries ago—Jeremiah states that these must be written in the dust of the ground. So, the Priests took to writing these incidents in the dust at the Nicanor Gate, just over there.'

Joseph pointed to the Temple entrance where Jesus was standing. 'Thus, while still recording the necessary details,' Joseph went on, 'it is not a permanent record to be used against them at a later date. These Scribes and Pharisees that you saw today know this, and when they saw this Jesus of Nazareth writing in the dust of the ground, they knew that He knew what was really going on! They knew how it would be conducted and recorded at the Temple by the Priests, and now they saw it being done in the same manner before them by this Prophet, right here.'

I pondered this for a moment, as I watched Jesus depart along with His disciples. I could see how so many at home would be brought before the Priests here in the very same way if they lived over there, and for the very same reasons. Luckily for me, our Druidic priests are different—no stoning for me.

As we walked on from that place, a puzzling detail arose in my mind? 'Why did Jesus write it down twice then?' I asked. 'Surely, once would be enough.'

Joseph then explained He did not write the same thing twice. 'When you are first brought before the Priests, you are to write down the name of the person who is charged with the offence, and then you must list the law that was broken— what they are charged with.' He sighed. 'This is what Jesus wrote down the first time, and then He stood up and asked for the first person who was without sin to cast the first stone.'

I nodded, remembering. Even with my poor grasp of the language, I'd caught that much.

'As they recognised that Jesus saw what they were trying to do—breaking the law themselves—they could not cast the first stone. To do so in such a time would have meant for them to be stoned as well. However, they persisted in asking for Jesus to call for stoning even after all of this, and so He wrote again in the dust. This time, He was required to write out the passage from Deuteronomy where it states that a matter is to be decided by the mouths of two or three witnesses, and then list their names. Now, in Judaic Law, there are specific ways of doing things, with specific results of those actions. For instance, if anyone is found guilty of giving false evidence or witness, even if this was found out at a much later date, and especially if someone lost their life by way of their testimony, then they are to be rounded up and stoned to death as well. These records were a way of knowing who to look for if this occurred.'

'It's a way of keeping everyone honest,' I said. That I understood.

'When Jesus again wrote in the dust, He wrote out the appropriate passage, but when He came to the part of listing the names of the witnesses, they all left.'

'They did not want their names recorded,' I deduced.

Joseph nodded and took a moment to catch his thoughts. 'Under our law, if there is no-one to charge you with an offence, regardless of whether you committed any crime or not, then you are free to go. They tried to trick Jesus by way of the law and how to apply it, but He answered them "through" the Law, and they were left without excuse.'

Can you see, my friend, how I find this all so strange? I find it difficult to wrap my thoughts around this, but it became worse when He told her to 'go and sin no more.' After having found out the definition and meaning of sin for the Jewish people, then I must confess it would be difficult, or even impossible, to stop all sinning. I must admit, it was not so bad when I thought about how we lived with our many gods back here. However, they believe in just ONE God, the Giver of the Law, and He guards it jealously. There are no other gods to blame, or to reach for when the going gets tough.

With that hanging over my thoughts, I don't know if I could do it at all, let alone how this woman was supposed to do it. It was such a tortuous exercise to think it even possible. Fortunately, Joseph came again to my rescue when I asked him. On this, he told me that Jesus was really only addressing her situation of 'living with another man who was not her husband.' He was telling her to go back to her father's house and do it right.

Joseph added that this was also a prophecy about us and God's Kingdom—go back to the Father's House, and get it right. Get back to the one God. I felt a strange lurch of the heart as he said that. I was in the same situation as the woman? Was that what Joseph was implying?

He went on to speak of the Kingdom of God, apparently a common teaching subject by Jesus of Nazareth. While I did not get to meet Him then, I was amazed at how He talked to those Priests. He did not back down as one defeated, or even of lower stature or rank. As I finished my time of trading in this magnificent city, I listened for stories about Jesus.

My purse was full to overflowing, the caravan loaded with new merchandise for sale on the journey home and, with every new story of Jesus that I heard, my heart was changing. I was starting to question myself about loving only my wife, and her only, for the rest of my days. I have not yet come to a full decision on this, but I hope you now understand why I am different after this journey. None other has touched my heart as this one did.

I also hope you do not judge me over my telling of it, for I do not know how to answer such things. I often wonder if I would ever have thought about this at all if it wasn't so strange, but now, because of its strangeness, its uniqueness, I cannot stop thinking about it. Adding to my burden is, now that I know their meaning of sin, I feel that I ought to start sorting out the attitudes and behaviours of my own life.

I am drawn to this Kingdom of God. So drawn. And that, perhaps, is the strangest thing of all.

Joseph's Dilemma
JO WANMER

Approximately 2,000 years ago

A Jewish town

'Joseph ! No! This is crazy.'

'But, Dad, the angel said...'

'Angel? It was only a dream. If you hadn't eaten so much pizza last night...' Joseph's father, Jacob, glared at his son.

Joseph's stomach churned. *What could he do now?* His father disagreed with God's message.

The early morning light glistened on Jacob's wet hair. 'Joe, you can't marry an adulteress, especially one who's pregnant!'

Joseph quietened his nerves. 'But God told me to go ahead.'

'What? You're saying God is asking you to marry a girl who isn't a virgin? Blasphemy!' Jacob threw his hands in the air. 'My God demands her stoning. Read the scrolls. We'd be the scorn of town. We are God-fearing people. I won't risk my position in the synagogue because of one silly dream.'

'I... I... I can't disobey God.'

'Rubbish, Joseph. God's law demands she be stoned for her sin. Get used to it.'

Something in Joseph snapped. 'That won't be happening, Dad. I will be bringing her here tomorrow, as planned.' As Joseph left the shed, he heard Jacob's hammer hit the workshop wall. His heart dropped. *What if he was wrong?*

He opened the kitchen door. 'Mum. I had a dream.'

Before she could even turn, one of his brothers yelled. She rushed from the kitchen.

Joseph grabbed his bowl, taking it outside. He sat on the step. Last night he'd intended to divorce his betrothed. This morning he felt he should marry her. Now he was confused. *What if the angel's words were true, as preposterous as they sounded? What if Mary was still a virgin and somehow God had done this?* He shook his head. Having studied the law all his life, he knew the passage the angel quoted. It was one of the Messianic passages, but he'd been taught the blessed woman chosen by God would be a virgin, but only until the point of conception. Any other interpretation of the Scripture was ridiculous, impossible.

His mother sank down beside him, a mug in hand. 'A dream? Tell me.'

'An angel told me to go ahead and marry Mary.'

'But son, God wouldn't ask you to do that. The community will shun you as well as her. You'd be punished for something you didn't do.'

'I feel as though it's an instruction from heaven.'

'Forget it, Joseph. Forget her. Write out divorce notices today.'

He trudged toward the synagogue, hoping to talk to his teacher. He needed someone, anyone, to agree with him, to stand with him. His heart felt as though it had been through a mangle. He'd finished the new room. It was time for the wedding celebrations to begin. Working on the room, he'd imagined arriving at Mary's door. Giggling bridesmaids would open it. He'd be very stern and demand his wife come.

He'd imagined the walk down the road with her hanging on his arm, so beautiful, young and innocent. A whole procession would follow—dancing, singing, laughing.

Now all his hopes were dashed. Mary had been away and returned with a baby bulging under her carefully draped dress. He'd seen her yesterday. She had lifted pleading eyes to his.

He had run away, shocked, brain whirling. Until then, he'd been the envy of other young men. Now he'd be the despised one.

At the synagogue, Mordecai stormed down the stairs. 'You're late! The plan's already in place. She will be stoned at the third hour.' Mordecai stalked off, his righteous nose high in the air.

Joseph sank onto a seat.

'Tough call, my friend.' The teacher he'd come to see touched him on the shoulder. 'I'm surprised. But come. Chin up! There are more girls growing up every day. Her sister looks good.'

'Can... can I talk? In private?'

The rabbi nodded and led the way up the stairs. Joseph was about to walk through the door when his heart faltered. What if the rabbi locked him in, wouldn't let him go home until it was too late, until they had taken her? Something told him that he mustn't confide in him.

'Sorry, Teacher.' He ran down the stairs, up a back street, over a fence and through a garden. It was the most direct route he knew.

He banged on her front door a day early. He wasn't dressed for a wedding. There wasn't a best man or friends of the groom.

Mary's mother opened the door a crack. Grief covered her face. Terror filled her eyes. He realised she thought he'd come to drag her to the stoning.

'Shalom. I've come for Mary. She is my wife. I will protect her from harm.'

'You still want her?' Her eyes were wide. The door opened. 'Mary. Come.'

She approached him smiling, yet tentative. 'Joseph. Thanks for coming. Can I explain?'

'Yes, but not until I have you safely home.' His heart leapt as her fingers curled around his hand.

He led her down back streets and across their neighbour's field. No one followed. No one danced. But she clung to his arm. She was young and beyond beautiful, for her face shone and her eyes sparkled. His heart sang.

'Joseph... You'll never believe it. I saw an angel...'

NONFICTION

An Angel in Nazareth

ANNE HAMILTON

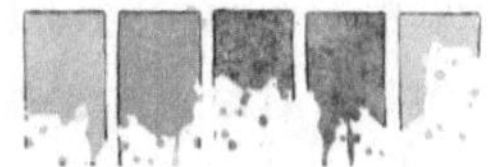

When I was in my late teens, I used to have a recurring nightmare. Wolves with human faces kept chasing me through my grandmother's house. I eventually discovered several hiding places where, for some baffling reason, they could never find me. They'd look in the door, sniff, and then, after a cursory glance around, they'd back away. They'd never enter to do a thorough check. If I could make it to the laundry or the shower space or the bathroom, I seemed to become invisible and unsmellable. But the wolves would lurk around the house—watching, knowing I'd have to come out from hiding sooner or later. I could only escape them if I timed it just right and made a wild dash for the front gate just as an angel driving a taxi pulled up outside. That was where the nightmares always ended—with my hand poised to open the taxi-door.

Taxi-driving angels are the stuff that dreams are made of. It's not an occupation you expect a heavenly being to engage in. It's a mix of the physical world and the spiritual realm that doesn't seem right or natural. At least, that's what I used to think...

But then I was visiting Israel. I'd never been before and didn't really know what to expect. It was spring but the temperature was unseasonably hot, much hotter in fact than summer back home in the sub-tropics. The tour days were long and tiring, and to complicate matters, I hadn't had any sleep on the trip over. I'd been awake most of the second night as well and, by the fourth day, I was exhausted. I was so pleased when we arrived in Nazareth for lunch and found it cooler and shadier.

Nazareth is, of course, famous as the hometown of Joseph and Mary. It's where Jesus grew up. Perched on a high ridge overlooking the Jezreel Valley, it's the largest city in the northern district of Israel and is considered the Arab capital of the nation. The majority of the population—around 70%—is Muslim and most of the remainder are Christians.

As our tour group entered the restaurant at Nazareth Village, sizzling flatbread was being baked in an open fireplace. Soon we were being treated to a meal similar to those from biblical times. Along with our warm fresh flatbread came dips of za'atar, hummus and labaneh. Za'atar is made of ground hyssop, sesame seeds, and olive oil; hummus was the usual chickpeas with tahini; and labaneh is yogurt and ground wheat. I had just finished sipping some water and was wondering if I could actually finish the last few bites of flatbread on my plate when an announcement was made that the main course of roast chicken was about to be served.

I stared at the flatbread in dismay, thinking: *There's more to come? Surely not.*

The next thing I became aware of was someone very close to my face and a voice, far too loud, saying, 'It's all good. It's ok. Her eyes are opening.'

I'd blacked out.

Apparently for the best part of two minutes. I'm told I slowly toppled backwards off the long bench seat, hit my head on the concrete with a crunch and splattered a reasonable amount of blood on the floor. Fortunately I was wearing a canvas hat that lessened the impact.

By the time I was conscious again, an ambulance had already been called and a couple of paramedics carted me off to the nearest hospital. Actually it was only a few hundred metres away and I could probably have walked there but no one was taking any chances. My good friend, Janice, accompanied me in the ambulance.

Now I wasn't entirely surprised by the turn of events. A few weeks earlier as I was contemplating the tour itinerary, God had said to me, 'You're going to hospital in Israel.'

My sense of there being no negotiation over this announcement was so strong I simply asked Him: 'How long for?'

And when I didn't get an answer, I decided to do something that was long, long overdue—I contacted a lawyer and made out a will. Just in case.

So there Janice and I were in the ambulance. We were taken just up the hill to the emergency department of the EMMS community hospital. There we were dropped off and we quickly discovered we were at a distinct disadvantage when it came to language. The staff were all fluent in Arabic and Hebrew. None of the signs were in English. While some of the staff understood English quite well, it wasn't at the level of a native speaker.

Now right at the start, we needed identification to register. Fortunately, I'd been advised to carry a photocopy of my passport page at all times. That was all I had, but it turned out to be sufficient by way of identification and documentation.

Although the hospital has been in operation since the mid-nineteenth century and is also known as the Scottish Hospital from its beginnings as a Christian outreach mission, the emergency department looked to be only about as old as I am. It had a 1950s feel to it and it radiated that sense of warm reassurance that's missing in modern facilities. Maybe it's just me but sterile, clinical-looking wards don't inspire confidence.

Janice and I were escorted through a labyrinth of pale green corridors to some seats where we waited for me to be called for x-rays and scans and tests. The doctors and technicians would peep out of doorways, look around, call, 'Marie…' When we didn't respond straight away, they'd come out, look at us in a vaguely puzzled way and say, 'Marie…?' again.

From the first, I knew they were looking for me but I was busy wondering why they were using my middle name.

Janice would say, 'Anne…' and they'd look at a paper and immediately revert to Marie. In retrospect, I think we managed to thoroughly convince them by this repeated show of incomprehension that my concussion was much more serious than it was.

Eventually it dawned on me why this mix-up with the names was happening. The medical staff all spoke Arabic and Hebrew and, in those languages, people read from right to left. Because my information had been taken from the photocopy of my passport page and not from a verbal registration, the first and middle names had been transposed.

After the testing was done, we were sent back through the labyrinth to a waiting area. And there we waited. An hour or so down the track, one of the staff told us we'd be able to go in half an hour. So Janice phoned the tour directors on the bus, asked where they were, and told them we'd catch a taxi and meet up with them on the way.

'No,' came the reply. 'We'll organise a taxi and send you the details.'

It hadn't really occurred to us to that point that, as tourists, we would be easy prey for unscrupulous operators. So we were grateful when the tour directors offered to find a reputable company for us and arrange for the pick-up. A few minutes later, the name of the driver and the taxi company was texted through to Janice.

Now hospitals being what they are, half an hour ticked past. And another half hour. And another. And another.

We were still waiting, unsure of what the hold-up was, when a man came into the waiting area, looked around, then walked right up to us. He asked—in English—if we were waiting for a taxi. He must have guessed who we were because we were the only obvious foreigners there.

Janice asked him if he was the person whose name she'd been given.

'No,' he said. 'He wasn't willing to wait any longer. He's gone. But don't worry, I'm here to take care of you.'

Now, you know, in all the old stories, angels clearly have a protocol for interacting with humans for the first time. 'Don't be afraid,' is one of their opening lines. So, if this man had said, 'Don't be afraid,' I might have been suspicious right then and there. Probably not that he was an angel but I would definitely have considered the possibility much earlier than I did. But, 'Don't worry,' has a more natural ring to it. Maybe it's the twenty-first century update on the ancient protocol.

Anyway, for the first time all afternoon, we were helped by someone with impeccable English. He also spoke Hebrew and Arabic and straight away he began liaising with the medical staff about my situation. It appeared, though we hadn't been told this, that the doctors wanted to conduct more tests— more scans and x-rays. The taxi-driver offered to take us back through the labyrinth to the right rooms and then, tests done, he conducted us back to the registration area.

There he once more liaised with the staff, discovered we had to sign a release document and, just as that was about to happen, he was informed that the doctors would prefer me to stay overnight for observation. He relayed all this to us. I said I would prefer to rejoin the tour. I just wanted peace and quiet, and I wasn't sure I'd get it in the hospital. Apparently my decision meant that a doctor had to come and personally explain the risks to me and get me to sign a waiver if I stuck to my decision. Eventually that happened—and while the doctor's English was quite good, the taxi-driver helped a few times along the way.

At last the papers were signed. All we had to do was pay and we could be off.

In retrospect, I think it was because I was leaving the hospital against medical advice that insurance wouldn't cover the costs. The trouble was, I had no money with me. I'd been whisked away from the restaurant without a credit card, passport or visa. I'd been fortunate to have that photocopy of my passport page tucked away.

Janice was more than happy to pay and be reimbursed later. The only problem was that none of her credit cards worked. Not one. Half a dozen futile attempts were made by the receptionist, including manual entry. We were wondering how to negotiate this impasse when the taxi-driver came up next to us, leaned over the counter and asked the receptionist, 'How much is it?'

'Six hundred shekels,' she answered.

Opening his wallet, the taxi-driver peeled off the bills and handed them over to her.

At this point Janice and I both realised something miraculous was going on. We should have been clued in previously, since the man's helpfulness and patience were far beyond the ordinary, but this was the too-good-to-be-true moment that took us both aback. We eyed each other. Nothing like this would ever happen back home in Australia. And we were pretty sure it never happened in Israel either. Wherever we'd been, people were looking out for the big tip, they weren't being expansively generous.

Who on earth was this man? As we went out to his taxi, we tried hard to find out. As he drove us through the peak-hour traffic of Nazareth, we asked questions hoping we'd find out more about him. As he took us by back routes to avoid obviously congested streets, we inquired about life in the city, hoping he'd tell us about himself. He did. But when it came to identification, we were at a loss. 'I belong to the family of the patriarch,' was the closest we came to eliciting personal information.

I decided there must be a Greek Orthodox cathedral in town—turns out it was St Gabriel's, *what else?*—and, as he drove past various churches I hoped we'd see that cathedral. In vain. A half hour or so we arrived in Sepphoris where the tour bus was waiting for us. The taxi fare, strangely, was much less than the ambulance fee that had been paid by our tour guide. We thanked the man with the deepest gratitude, repaid his expenses and waved good-bye. He drove off into the twilight as Janice and I boarded the bus.

It was only the next day, when I had time to think about all that had happened that I began to wonder about the man. There suddenly came to mind those dreams from more than four decades in the past of being rescued from wolves by a taxi-driving angel.

Oh, but surely not, my rational mind protested.

The part of me that believes in miracles put up an immediate counter-protest, reminding me of the strangeness of it all. I began to be suspicious about that statement: 'I belong to the family of the patriarch.' Was this an ecclesiastical title, or did he mean Abraham—a rather cunning answer in an Arab city within a Hebrew-speaking nation—or was it a heavenly Patriarch he was referring to?

In the end, I decided that, even if the taxi-driver wasn't an angel, then he was most definitely an agent of divine providence.

But suspicion still floated in and out of my thoughts. After all, where else in the world would anyone be more likely to meet an angel than in Nazareth?

A Sidetrack to Damascus

i.m. Alison Cotes

ROSS CLARK

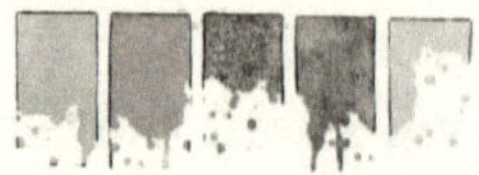

1 CONVERSION

Never had one—at least not in the way
the word is usually meant: no blinding light,
no falling of scales from eyes, no burning
crosses in the sky, nor even St Elmo's Fire
(though I should have liked the artistry
of that), no choirs of angels, no glossolalia
Hallelujahs, nothing like that at all.

Rather, it was someone ordinary asking me
outright one day what I had never been asked
before in my life, and as I answered in a
somewhat shaky affirmative what I'd never
quite known about myself, I heard the gears
of two wills beginning to engage together, and
a small voice all around me saying *So be it.*

2 AFTERWARDS,

I still put on the same old clothes
every day, never finding the need for
sackcloth and ashes, nor other such
penitential garments of allegiance;

those who knew assured me that I
would soon wear beneath my clothes
more subtle and chafing hair-shirts
that mortal eyes would never see.

My life was not in dramatic change,
but gradually some of the old ways
healed over as the water and the wine
washed clean my patient limbs.

3 GRACE

Though I hardly ever pause to give
thanks at meals, I think I know
the reason now—why only food?

Why not also health of limb
and breath, restful sleep,
the comfortable passion of sex,

the joy to the eyes of clouds
and rocky slopes and whatever
else appeals? Music perhaps?

Surely I'm not to spend all
my life in praising You for things
done and things partaken,

at the cost of further doing
and partaking? Time enough
in Heaven for continual and

deserved praise! I live now,
and promise to enjoy all that
I am yet to receive; so take

these words as my thanks,
delivered to, and in presence of,
Your folk assembled here.

HEALING

Yesterday's cut has begun
to heal already: the flap
of skin that wept all day
has crusted overnight,

as gradually and as
certainly as the turning
of this green planet.

Although no eye can see
it happening, the miracle
continues in today's
broad light, with red-
ness, swelling, hardening.

By next month, only a
thin white scar will mark
the site of the skirmish
between my body's platoons
and the infective snipers
of my unseen opposition.

The spirit too heals
in just such a manner—
with the certain turning
of this familial earth.

5 LENTEN

I have given up nothing this Lent,
but so many things are giving me up.

All my bills are overdue,
all my invoices unanswered.

I have worked my way down
to the generic groceries
and the change tin.

I have not had my medications
for weeks, and they will take weeks
to kick in again.

Even drink is not an option
till my next dole payment.

My friends cry off engagements
at the last moment, or don't call back.

Whenever I go anywhere,
everyone looks at me twice,
then looks away.

Let me add:
the last batch of blades was faulty,
and I've used them too many times:
my face and head are covered with cuts.

Forgive me.

Let me not betray You
            with these vain comparisons.

Let me not deny You
            with this addendum to Job.

Let me not crucify You
            with these irrelevant truths.

ADVENT...

(Jacarandas are covert as Christians
living unnoticed amongst us
until their season blooms them
into the purple unseamed robes
of their mocked Master. All year
we do not see them, and then,
suddenly, they are a crowd
that flings blossoms at our feet
and sings *Hosanna! Hosanna!*

How bright and intense they are,
until drab Summer drains us
and Fall returns: multitudes await
their coming again as if it were
life itself we waited for, hoped for.)

6 CRUX

I read that there are 88 constellations:
then I find that they are numbered
from the brightest, the prime,
to the dimmest, our own Crux,
at 88 the least amongst equals,
sufficient though for our first flag.

Invisible by day in the sky,
it is forever on my skin,
etched red with that other cross
of my northern dreamings,
and the other totems of my heart.

They are my strength and my consolation.

In darkness I orient myself by first
turning south, thence the east that
I shall face forever. One day,
under the faintest constellation
of a cross invisible by day
through the bluest sky
(raucous with the melodies of birds),
and in the moist earth that is my mater
and my matter and my legacy,
my brine-blue eyes shall close at last
and I shall rest.

And my offspring shall erect a cross
to my height, and thus not quite
to the depth of my burying, and
I shall rest beneath it, on my grace
of feathers, with Crux light-years above me,
Crux inked on my arm, and Crux burned
on my heart, where nobody sees though
everybody knows, and I shall find
the sky's faintest light sufficient then,
                as now, to my rest and my salvation.

Faith and Grief

PAMELA JULIAN

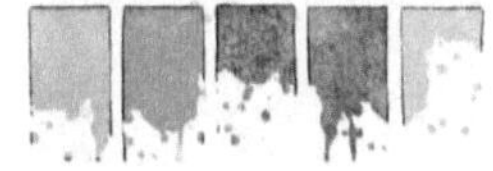

'We might need to look at a cochlear implant.'

I couldn't reply.

'Can you come back for a series of hearing tests? Book a two-hour session.'

I left the audiologist's and went home and cried. And cried. For four months.

A cochlear implant already? I didn't expect this for another five years.

I knew my hearing aid wasn't helping much as I often took it out of that ear and relied on my 'good' ear. But I did not realise that it was because I had rapidly lost almost all of my remaining hearing in that ear.

And so the battery of tests started. 'When you hear the sound, push the button.' I listen. *Was that a beep?* Both ears; then one ear; then the other. By the end of two hours, I was pressing the button randomly. The prelude to a cochlear implant is extensive—hearing tests, speech recognition tests, MRI, CT Scans, visits to the surgeon, the audiologist, back to the surgeon. And eventually to the operating theatre.

Then the Big Day. It gets Turned On. I'd read about people who cried with joy when theirs was turned on. My experience was more like visiting Mars: *Baarp. Barrp Ping. Tinkle. Ba-a-arp.*

I kept a diary:

DAY 2

I got up and sat outside with a coffee. The first thing I heard was a crow's voice squawking in the rhythm of a dove—*barp-ba-a-rp bup*. Put my hearing aid in the other ear to check that it was in fact a dove. Yay! My first identified sound.

Then I heard a crow—*ba-a-ar-p ba-ar-arp* (which is what everything sounds like with the cochlear implant anyway).

So, now I can talk to the birds.

DAY 5

Applied little green man to my ear.

Oh dear. Music sounds like gargling underwater.

Wow, the world is noisy! I can hear the hot water system gurgling—I think. The trouble is I haven't heard that noise for so long with my good ear, that when I put my hearing aid in to try to identify it, I still can't be sure.

4 WEEKS

All cochlear implant packages should come with a label. *Warning: this device causes strange behaviour.*

I'm sure my neighbours think I'm weird—I stand outside with my finger in one ear, listening to the wind and leaves rustling. I asked the council worker at the park if I could stand and listen to the lawn mower to learn the sound…

Cars approaching from a hundred metres or so sound like water dribbling into the toilet, then turn into a hoarse grunt as they pass by.

Rehab is basically learning every sound again, as it now flows through the cochlear implant. Every sound: a tap running, the kettle boiling, my sleeve brushing across the page as I write, computer keys tapping, car indicators. Every. Single. Sound.

So I'm keeping a record, because as I learn them, I can file them away into 'background sounds'. I recognise some sounds by the rhythm—bird-song, phone ringing, impact drill.

I've identified a few:

- Breathing is like four or five tinkling bells
- Wind blowing is like whop whop down a cardboard tube
- Microwave pings are like two plastic spoons tapping together
- Kettle boiling is like being underwater in a spa.

As one of my friends said, 'This will either eventually make sense, or you will have a wonderfully imaginative life!'

I have also had plenty of time for reflection. I'm not discouraged exactly, but I have struggled with deteriorating hearing loss for over forty years. I've been working at 100% to hear what people say for the last 10–15 years, and I'm tired. I'm weary of the struggle to hear. I'm tired of listening so hard even during the simplest interaction—like buying milk.

And sad. I've watched my life get smaller as I've dropped activities because I can't hear well enough to participate in them. I've changed the way I interact socially to accommodate my ever-decreasing ability to hear. No more meetings; no plays or concerts; no noisy restaurants. I can't even hear speech when I'm walking beside someone. And the financial cost—friends have holidays; I have hearing aids. Friends work full-time; I am only able to manage part-time due to listening fatigue.

I have experienced the chronic grief that goes with a disability—and especially where the disability worsens. I have wept buckets as I've lost yet another ability—like hearing music. And I have often asked God, 'Why?' I've asked for prayer many times, and yet I still have deteriorating hearing.

Anyone with a disability will be able to tell you about the daily struggle just to do what other people can do easily; the impact on quality of life; and the fatigue associated with the struggle. They will also tell you that most equipment and aids do not *fix* the problem—they merely *alleviate*. They may provide opportunity to access things that otherwise would be unavailable but, at best, there remains a deficit in function. And this can be significant. For example, I would really struggle with doing an online course if it is not captioned, even with all my assistive devices.

Initially, my hearing was worse in the early post-operative months. I have two different devices. One is acoustic—anyone who wears hearing aids will tell you that it isn't quite the same as 'normal' hearing. But that cochlear! It is mechanical; it is ping-y and ting-y; it is soft for loud sounds, then really loud. Voices are much higher pitched, and it takes weeks of practice to identify if it is a man or a woman speaking. Identifying the words spoken is not even on the radar at this point. I am listening to a different sound in each ear. All the time.

At one point, my kind audiologist asked me if I'd thrown it across the room yet. 'Close,' I said. 'Very close.' (I do know one girl who did!) I leant on that poor audiologist for support, and cried at him. I think he could tell how things were going by my face as soon as I walked in the room. And also when things were finally improving.

I'm now around 18 months post-op. It's still a work in progress, but it is easier.

Do I enjoy having a cochlear implant? I think *enjoy* is too strong a word, but it sure beats the alternative. And yes, I would do it again. My isolation has lessened as my understanding of sounds has improved, and I am working part-time with an amazing group of people. I have found a fabulous cochlear support group, and value the friendship of these people—some of whom struggle more than I do. They come from all walks of life—pilots, musicians, missionaries.

I grieve over the loss of so much in my life, especially as I acquired a second disability many years ago. I felt my life shrink even more, to a tiny fraction of what it used to be. It was hard to give up the many active pursuits I love. I am learning to live with restrictions, and with grief. Is it easy? No. Would I love healing? More than I can say!

I have often wondered what my life would have been like if I had been well, and if I could hear. I have friends who accomplish so much! Instead, I wonder what I am to 'do' with my life with so many limitations. I've brought this before God many times. A few years ago, I started some of the gentle arts—writing, painting, embroidery—and have had a number of written works published. I am realising that God is not constrained by my shortcomings, and He has a different view of my abilities than the world does. In His graciousness, He has provided opportunities to develop other areas. Creative expression in writing, stitching and painting is not diminished by limited hearing.

The Brillianteer

DONNA ALBRECHT

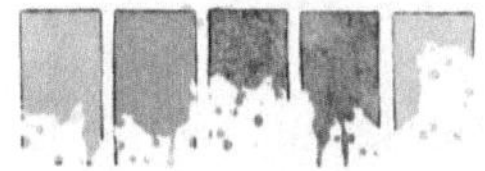

I quickly realise if I am going to be of any help, we will both need to be naked. Mum has been scratching her scalp all day. She never could tolerate dirty hair. I'm sure she's been lying there, visualising herself washing it. But it's no longer a possibility; she can barely stand now. 'I can help, Mum,' I offer.

A few days earlier, Mum had attended an oncology appointment, and was immediately admitted into Palliative Care. Major organs were shutting down. Rather than causing distress, this sudden move brought her relief: *they're finally listening, and doing something about my pain.*

I steady her as she collapses onto the plastic shower chair. Then I remove my clothes and put them on the too-small vanity unit. For a moment I see us, as if from the ceiling: our soft pale flesh blended together, in the middle of a cold grey room.

Her gold ruby ring sparkles as water washes over it. It's not her wedding ring. It appeared mysteriously, long after she had divorced. I never asked her about it. Streams of water flow over Mum's head, down her breasts, and pool in her lap. I chase away the shampoo bubbles with the handheld showerhead. She coos with enjoyment.

'Do it again,' she says.

'I can't, Mum,' I say gently, after the second wash, 'You'll have no oils left on your scalp.'

'Oh, it feels so nice,' she says.

'Mmm.' I smile. I can hardly take in what is happening. It feels strange to be this close to her.

She hadn't wanted children, and had told us so many times. By age twenty-one, she'd had three of us, before her doctor suggested The Pill. But I figured out early on that she liked me better if I helped her. I have flickering memories of the day I tried to clean up after my sister, who had dirtied her nappy, stepped out of it, and smeared its contents all over the walls. Little Helper Donna had grabbed clean nappies from the linen cupboard. I had expected Mum to be pleased, but instead, her look knocked the breath out of me. She couldn't tolerate tears. I hid away inside myself.

Over the decades, I became practiced at being the family peacekeeper, the good girl, the listener, the one who didn't talk back. When I left home at eighteen, I thought: *I can finally be myself*. I was confused when life followed the same patterns. I started to resent being the silent listener, the observer, the one who was invisible for others. Yet when the call came through that Mum is in Palliative Care, I dropped everything to be at her side.

On the plane, I imagine scenes from movies—the death-bed turnaround, the life-changes-in-an-instant story, where the characters speak their truth and forgiveness through tears…

When I walk into the hospital room, Mum says in a dry monotone, 'Oh, you're here.' Then she launches into a stream-of-consciousness mind-dump. It's business as usual. She talks and I listen.

At night I sleep beside her hospital bed. I'm often lying awake in the semi-darkness, watching her restless movements, her moaning, her gasping for air. I reach out and touch her hand, to reassure her. Her elegant hands are weathered with age. I remember her Sunday night ritual when I was a child, putting on deep plum-red nail polish at the kitchen bench. She stopped wearing it when chemo started. That was years ago. She stopped work and her life also stopped.

A number of times I call the nurse. She checks her vital signs and gives her more medication. Sometimes she simply says she is doing OK. *OK for someone who is dying, I think.*

In the early hours of morning, Mum starts to tell me stories—ones I've never heard before, about great losses and the pain she's held inside for decades. She tells me of the abortion clinic. How she waited outside for Dad to bring the money, to get rid of me. But Grandpa comes instead, and tells her that Dad will 'do the right thing'.

I don't react to this new information about me. I long ago learned to push this aside. The Peacekeeper smooths things over, so I don't feel anything. I care more about how others feel. In the quietness of night she unburdens her soul. I listen. I see where her hurt and bitterness have come from. But the fairytale-ending movies haunt me. It is not going the way I hoped. I'm not able to be anyone different in her presence. *What do I do?* I pray.

Then, one night, she wakes calling out to me, 'Donna. Donna.' She looks at me as if peering out from a long tunnel. 'Something's different,' she says emphatically. Then she is silent.

'Is it good different? Or bad different?' I ask.

She's tentative. 'All the noise in my head is gone.' I can see she's trying to process something deep and strange to her. Something about her face reminds me of a dream I had twenty years earlier—a figure dressed in glowing white standing before me in a dream. I tell Mum that it was Jesus and how, after that dream, life changed and I began to get peace then too. Her eyes are wide but she doesn't reply. Eventually we both return to sleep. The next day we have our time in the shower together. Water flowing between us. Something is different. The doctor tells Mum her organs are now stable enough for her to return home. I go back to Adelaide.

For the next four months we speak daily over the phone. 'What are you doing today?' she asks.

'Nothing special,' I say.

'That doesn't matter. Just talk to me.'

So I talk about cooking dinner, the washing, what I have to do the next day, and I even venture to tell her my worries. She listens. *Do I finally have the gift of a mother who wants to know me?* God reminds me that a year earlier He'd said, *I am redeeming family.*

During the weeks after leaving hospital, Mum takes more and more Fentanyl to dull the pain. She tells me how tired she is. The next day she takes an ambulance back to Palliative Care.

This time when I fly up to Brisbane and arrive at Palliative Care, she's not able to speak. All the medications pushed her into sedation. Her swallow reflex has stopped, she can no longer eat or drink. This time my sister sits at her bedside.

Mum is restless, and tries to get out of bed. She wants to be conscious, to say something. She holds on. On day four, I go to her home for a shower, but am called back urgently. My sister, Mum's ex-husband and his daughter, and Mum's housekeeper stand around the bed. *Why doesn't the house-cleaner leave us alone for our last moments with Mum?* I'm confused to see her link hands with Mum's ex across Mum's body.

Mum still doesn't let go. Perhaps she's waiting for my brother to be here. He's already said good-bye.

I ask around the room if I can pray. 'Let go, Mum… into Jesus' arms.' Her breath stops instantly. A guttural cry pours out of me, 'Mummy. Mummy.' *Be quiet. You're making too much noise*, I tell myself. I cry as I never have before.

Mum's ex-husband reaches over and takes the ruby ring off Mum's finger. 'Mum wanted Donna to have that ring!' my sister says loud enough for everyone to hear. He reaches stiffly across and begrudgingly places it in my hand. I put it on my finger. *My hands are like hers, but with shorter fingers. Why hadn't I noticed this until now?*

'I'm going to have to contest the Will,' Mum's ex-husband announces, the night before her funeral.

A small voice whispers, 'It will be a Moses and Pharaoh battle.' I'm thankful for the insight, but daunted by what this implies. *How many plagues and pestilences were there?* I wonder as I catch my breath… But it's also an assurance that God will fight this battle, and we will see our inheritance. And I already have the ring, like a promise. A reminder that Mum wanted to bless me. To bless her children. *She was different after our time in hospital.*

I've heard it said, 'It's a legal system, not a justice system.' For two and half years, my siblings and I are dragged down into the pits of the past. Yet, over and over, whispers of encouragement give me the strength to believe that it will all work out ok. I want to say that God's words kept me sure and strong, but as time drags on, I feel battered and powerless. I am weary. Fear floods through me.

When the ring catches my eye, it brings dark questions with no answers: *Why do we have to fight for an inheritance that should be ours? Was Mum lying to us all along? Didn't she care about us? How can you let us be abused all over again, God?* One day, I pull the ring off my finger and push it into the cavity behind a drawer.

And I close the drawer on my heart too. God can speak to my mind, but I don't trust anyone with my heart now.

As thoughts run freely during my morning shower, I wonder why Mum hadn't protected us. I chew over her fifteen years of slow descent into death. *Why didn't she fight? She kept her heart closed to us and blamed us for all of her hardships. Then she just gave up.*

At least I'm not like her.

Suddenly, it's as if the shower runs cold. *I think I'm better than she was. But I'm just like her.* If it weren't for The Peacekeeper and The Listener in me, I too would have poured out the same monologues and judgments as she did. My stomach convulses as I recognise we are two of a kind.

Was she the peacekeeper with both my Dad and her ex-husband? Was all of that talking her fight to find a voice and a place? Am I just the next in line of generation after generation appointed for rejection and abuse? Blaming others has stopped us realising our role in inflicting the same on the next generation. I feel the water washing over my head and my heart throbs with the truth of it. It's then I hear God's gentle voice again: *I have come to redeem your family.*

I realise: *it has to start with me.*

But how? I've tried so hard to be good, God, but I can't *overcome it.* I had tried so hard to be the loving one in the family. To not react to the evils. Be the nice Christian example. But as I see the extent of lifetimes of judgments, I realise how my heart has become so calloused. As I towel myself dry, I realise I have only shaved one leg.

I want God to clean up my heart, but after almost three years of turning away from Him, He speaks to me any way He can. As I sit quietly one morning, allowing Him to bring knowledge, but not get too close to my heart, he reveals the work of a Brillianteer—the specialist gem-cutter. The one who knows how to cut facets into stone. Gem-cutting styles change over time, but the purpose is the same: to arrange the facets in such a way as to allow light to penetrate into the depths of the stone, and reflect the fullness of light out again.

In my heart, I hear God say: *We need to go deeper if I'm to bring more light into your heart.* My eyes sting with tears as His presence speaks right to the core of my aching heart.

God begins to highlight words in my mind: things I've believed at my very core—all lies. Lies about life, about family, about God. *Mum will love me, if I'm her helper. We'll be safe, if I can smooth things over. I must keep the peace. I shouldn't be alive.* I begin to see the line of rejection, passed down from mother to child. The curses that sought to destroy the children over generations. I notice the strategies I found to hide away my pain, and keep myself safe. *Keep quiet. Don't bring attention to yourself. Be good. Make sure everyone is happy. Don't speak. Don't cry.* I wished to be invisible, but couldn't know the devastating consequences of this—I had abdicated my life. God brings revelation after revelation until I am full and heavy from it. I sit with it.

What do I do with this, Lord?

You know I can't make myself any different.

But I still believe that You can.

And He does.

One afternoon, I sit in a room with three women, God's midwives of sanctification. I wonder how anyone could make sense of the tangled knot of thoughts and feelings I lay before them. Generations of lies, vows, curses of death. They guide me through prayers of forgiveness, breaking off lie after lie, renouncing the decisions that had led to darkness and death. The wedge that has stopped love from flowing from mother to daughter, words spoken that had cut off joy and life purpose, and identity. Each piece a weight lifted. Until I sit with peace.

'I always ask Father God what He'd like to say or give at the end of a prayer session,' one of the women says quietly. 'I see Father God giving you a gold ring, with a large red stone.' My eyes sting and blur with tears. *You're giving me back Mum's ring, God.*

I'm relieved the ring is still there when I search for it, and put it back on my finger. *Now it shines light that carries love in it.* God shows me again a vision He gave me just weeks after Mum's death. Jesus holds a newborn baby in His arms. It is Mum.

I had thought that redeeming my family meant some kind of Superman act, where Jesus would show up. I'd be Jesus' sidekick, just following everything He said with a loud: 'Yeah. That's it, Jesus.'

And my family's hearts would immediately open to God for healing. But redeeming family is a deep and bloody business, just like it was for Jesus. And just like Him, we are broken open in the process—wounds washed with blood and water.

I catch the light of the ruby beaming back a bright red sparkle. It reminds me that Mum loved me the best she could. God can heal all the places where she couldn't. I realise that, when Jesus said He would fight for us, for our inheritance, He wanted to give us much more than the money and possessions passed on to the next generation. He wants us to have more of Him. More of the undoing all that has darkened our hearts, if we will surrender it to Him. He is rewriting our history and our heritage.

Now when I glimpse the ruby ring, I'm reminded that Jesus is the Brillianteer, bringing light deep into my family. It has started with my heart, and now I partner with Him to shine it out to my family.

Justen's Story

From child soldier in Sudan to God's soldier in Brisbane

RUTH BONETTI *with* JUSTEN WANI NASONA

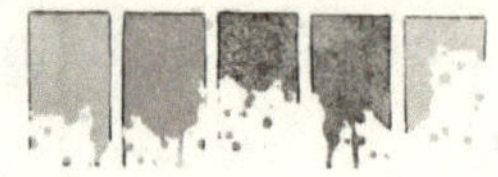

A high voltage smile, white on black, radiates God's love and faith in His protection. Intrigue follows my first impression of Justen Nasona. I ask how his faith withstood traumatic experiences as a 13-year-old soldier in Sudan. Abducted from his school by rebel freedom fighters, the Sudan People's Liberation Army. Taken to a training camp where he and some friends adjusted to homesickness, a cold jungle with just a bare blanket and bare feet. There was little food to survive, but Justen's father Nasona, a skilled hunter, had taught his son to kill gazelles, monkeys, baboons and pythons.

'I used to hunt with a team of three or four people and bring back food for the entire barracks.'

Aged 18, in a dark night of the soul, Justen lay wounded on a battlefield amongst fifty dead bodies, until rescued at dawn.

Nasona taught his son more than hunting skills. Justen quotes his father's sustaining words:

To die in Christ is a better life and takes you to the kingdom of God. Be strong in faith, look forward and continue in the work of God. If you die, you will meet your family later.

Justen was born into a Christian family on 1 January 1975 in Wonduruba, a suburb of Juba, Central Equatoria, South Sudan. Predominantly Christian, the religions were Church of England and Catholic. The youngest and a favourite of the ten siblings, he was named Just-ten by his father Nasona Kwaje Younga. His older sister, who was number seven, took care of Justen, carrying him on her back to fetch water from the river. At the age of seven, Justen's parents placed him in primary school from 1981 to 1986. In 1989 he completed intermediate school.

That year, the military seized power, and Justen's life changed. He pointed to a photo of two lanky young men outside their thatched hut.

This is me with my cousin, Samiel, before we went to the second battle together. He didn't come back. I was badly injured. See, that's me being put into a helicopter.

Sudan was under joint British-Egyptian rule until 1955, gaining independence in 1956. War had raged between Christians and Muslims until 1972. It erupted again in 1983 when President Gaafar Nimeiry declared Sudan an Islamic state, revoking the autonomy of the majority Christian SSAR. This propelled the country into the Second Sudanese Civil War; the government campaigned against the people of South Sudan—Muslims against Christians.

If I chose to convert to Muslim I could stay; if not, I must go and fight. How can you raise a family in the Muslim way? It's a rigid system. Much doesn't go well, must learn the way of living, of prayer, customs. A husband cannot even see his wife's eyes.

Led by Dr. John Garang De Mabior, the rebels aimed to overthrow the old regime—the government of Sudan—so the Christians might regain freedom of speech, regardless of race, gender, or religion. More than 1.2 million people died.

The rebel leader, a doctor and professor, recruited young boys because they didn't know anything. If you want to be a Christian, you go join the war; you fight and at the end you have free school— if you survive.

For ten months Justen was trained in Cuba to learn to drive and operate tanks, and to activate an anti-missile controller. Back home, he was thrust into the war which broke out in 1990—the Arabs against the Christian South and the Indigenous people of the country. To the present day, the country is divided into Sudan and South Sudan.

Justen points to his photographs atop a tank, boarding a helicopter when wounded, and says:

My memory of 1989 and 1990 is of danger, death, injury. Sometimes I was afraid but I know that God was with me. He has kept me going until today.

WOUNDED IN ACTION

In 1989 the military seized power. Heavy fighting between Sudan and South Sudan continued through 1990 until 1991. Survival was uncertain.

I didn't know what might happen. Our unit had five tanks and one night we lost three, including mine. Missiles would take 10–30 seconds to explode, so we needed to scamper from there, me and the operator.

Justen crawled out of the tank just before it blew up—and escaped into the path of the bullets. He attempted to run, but he was dizzy from a head wound. His leg was broken.

We started fighting at 7 pm, and people were dying all around, more than fifty bodies. Because the battle erupted at night and there was smoke everywhere, I couldn't run away. It was horrible. I was crying but I don't know where the tears came from. Everywhere I saw people lost but I still survived. Then around 4 am I saw a person walking forwards with a gun. I decided if he's my enemy let him kill me. When I recognised our uniform, I tried to move toward. But I was badly injured in the head and leg. He whistled for help. I was carried to the barracks health unit.

When asked if he could operate tanks again, Justen said no.

I was traumatised. I decided to escape and seek a new life away from the army. In 2000 I wrote for a discharge to leave the army. I thank God he kept me alive until I got to Australia.

While still a young lad, Justen had been selected to be an army chaplain and would pray and bless everyone before they went into the battle. Justen's nickname 'Didi' means *the bomber*. His fellow soldiers would say, 'Didi, come and bless everybody here.'

Justen raised his hand up and prayed:

God, we are fighting for our soil, we are not fighting to kill anybody, but we are defending our country, our green lands and mountains and river, not to be taken by Arabs. Physically we are going forward, under Your cover.

He laughed.

Everybody called 'Wooo!' This prayer gave us energy to go forward in power. And I still continue to go on in the work of God. From that time till now, if I miss a Sunday to worship, it feels like one month.

MARRIAGE AND DEATHS

A friend suggested Justen meet Joice Keji from another town; they became engaged in 1986.

But there was no contact—no kissing!

They married 11 years later in 1997, while he was home on leave in his home village. It was a traditional ceremony wearing the clothing of their culture.

Joice's father gave her to my father who gave her to me. She didn't know I was a soldier. Because when I took leave, I must leave everything there, show no sign of army.

In the community, people thought Justen's father sent him to school somewhere. He disappeared for ten years.

I was fighting in the north-east, more than four days' drive away by truck or by car. Nobody would get there because of the fighting. People looked for me in our homeland but thought maybe I was in Ethiopia or Khartoum.

'Why didn't you tell me?' Joice asked after they married and she saw his army uniform.

Justen replied, 'For security. My family couldn't tell anything. It doesn't matter. That's part of life.'

Both mothers died. In 1999, Justen's mother Yunish Nyoka fell ill but there was no opportunity for hospital in a season of war. A brother was very sick, but recovered. Another brother died in battle, and cross-fire killed his father Nasona in 2000. Justen felt deep loss.

Dad was orphaned at around ten years old but the community took care of him. In order to afford marriage and raise a family, Nasona became a hunter. He was a tall, gentle, kind and smart man, brown-skinned and not black like me. The best place to hunt was the savannah forest west of Juba. Using metal wire snares, bows and arrows or Uganda machine guns, Dad killed many animals such as gazelles, pigs, antelopes, lions, elephants, monkeys, baboons and crocodiles. He hid the hunting tools so that the children didn't get into trouble. Because I was the youngest, he began to trust and teach me from age ten until I joined the army in 1986. To catch an animal can be simple. But you need to aim for the right place on the animal's body.

Struggling amidst the challenges of war, with no parents left, Justen knew that survival lay in a refugee camp—they could not endure in Southern Sudan.

STRUGGLE TO THE KAKUMA REFUGEE CAMP

The couple journeyed from Wonduruba to Yei River then to Uganda. Three weeks later they crossed the border to arrive in 2001 at the Kakuma Refugee camp in the Turkana area of Kenya. Five brothers and sisters went to a refugee camp, where four remain. His sisters are all lay preachers, one a pastor, another a deacon. A brother migrated to America.

Living in a tent, their four years there were challenging but they endured. Justen thanks God for His unconditional love and protection. Yet this was not the place for the children they so desired.

EXODUS FROM THE REFUGEE CAMP

The commander offered a form for resettlement to Australia. They were called for an interview which was successful and after just a few days their visas came through. On 26 November 2005, they took a bus to Nairobi and next day flew from Nairobi to Australia.

We landed on the 28 November 2005, arriving at Brisbane airport at 5 am. When we touched Australian soil, I told my wife, this is an unbelievable miracle. We were filled with happiness. I couldn't believe that the community was so welcoming. After settling in, we could afford to raise a child.

A decade later, my daughter-in-law met refugees arriving in the early hours, in her role as a Humanitarian Settlement Services Case Manager. How her warm smile would have uplifted many similarly exhausted and war-weary refugees!

FAMILY LIFE IN BRISBANE—AUSTRALIA

The couple longed for a family but a futile 11 years dragged on. Joice despaired, almost near to leaving. People marry to have children. African society has little respect for childless couples. When they arrived in Australia, Justen told Joice, 'Now we will get a child.' But working for a company full time seven days a week did not help. A doctor referred him to IVF.

At last God answered their prayers. Faith was conceived with IVF assistance, followed by natural births. Now Justen and Joice have five beautiful children; Faith Gale Justen, born in 2008; Nyoka Halelluia Justen, (2009); Ludiya Yeno Justen, (2011); Blessing Pita Justen, (2012); and Emmanuel Amen Justen, born in 2014. God had a plan and then after that:

Bang, bang, bang and we tried to stop!

Why God did you block this before? He's telling me back: God had a plan. If I had children in Africa we wouldn't be here. God blocked that way for children until it was safe in Australia.

What life means to me is a combination of so many things. This includes challenges that I went through day after day and night after night. Sometimes I think these challenges were all God's plan and design to protect me. Hence, my mission is to come to God and praise Him and start my real life in Jesus Christ. My father and mother called me Justen Wani (meaning 'important leader'). From early days they told me: 'One day you shall be a leader somewhere. We see wisdom in you.' These words have encouraged me, and it shows me now that my leadership journey has just started.

Justen has become well known and respected in his community's place of worship and has led a group of Bari fellowship for six years.

God has opened the door for me and chose me among the number of people within the Bari Christian fellowship. The community is now asking me to do vocational training at a college.

He entered St Francis College as a formation student in 2022, preparing for the ministry. He serves at Bari Fellowship and enjoys its traditional Anglican ways of life in Brisbane, Australia.

Now life goes on with my family as we live and work in our new community homeland.

The Australian government does not recognise Justen's many African qualifications so he must begin again. He must also learn English. Justen speaks four languages; Bari, Arabic, Moro, Swahili.

English is so hard, so many colloquialisms. But if my brain is holding four languages, why not English? When I had an accident at work, I thank God for that. My wife encouraged me to go to TAFE, do something with my life.

'We see your brilliant smile now,' I say. 'How did that 13-year-old feel? The nearly-19-year-old?'

I did cry by myself back then. Now when it's me talking my story I want to cry, but for joy! Look at these photos, this is life in Australia. Now it's a glorious life, like being in heaven. School is free, no people fighting in the street or killing.

Justen's infectious smile illumines his face.

My dream is to tell everyone about our wonderful God.

A Sign

DIANA DAVISON

The opening of international borders propelled my personal life into uncertain territory. My world began to operate in jumpstart motions of interruptions and interspersed travel. COVID had taken a large toll on everyone. Now time seemed to move along at warp speed. Every ten weeks or thereabouts, I swapped one tropical climate—Queensland, Australia—for another—Sarawak, Borneo.

Each visit to this semi-sleepy state is to support my mother during the sunset of her life. These solo trips also acted to rekindle the bond of mother and daughter. I knew this latest wandering would not differ from the last—a rough rollercoaster with more downs than ups. Updates on her mental and physical wellbeing came regularly. And in each trip, the sensitive sorting of a lifetime of her hoarded possessions became an ongoing endeavour. This mountainous feat was upsetting and depressing. Sort, savour, save or sling? Belongings that told her story.

The many undertakings in this grief-worn situation overtaxed my brain. Unfortunately, it was turning out to be the norm of my existence. My frail mother, 86 years old, was experiencing a decline in health. She had been diagnosed with a spreading stage IV cancer. No opportunity existed for sight-seeing excursions on these sojourns. Any 'me-time' came at the end of the day in the privacy and solitude of my hotel room.

Every visit amounted to a daunting and draining fortnight. Regrettably, my mother needed to be transported to the hospital within two days of my return to my family. And so, once back on Australian home ground, I had a strong desire to escape myself, to leave the heavy mind luggage behind.

Three weeks later, I eventually took a long weekend at the coast to relax, rest and reset.

Getting away brought a sense of relief. After a late Saturday lunch, the vast stretch of coastline beckoned. *A walk on the beach will do me good*, I thought. *Clear the head*. It would put a pause on my private project of sorting out my household. *Declutter and rearrange belongings*.

I spent the last fifteen months, over each journey, physically doing this laborious task for my parent. It was time I did it for myself. The need to reduce any burden on my children, should anything happen to me, became the driving force. I knew how emotional and exhausting the entire circumstance can be.

As I strolled barefoot on the inviting golden grains, I noticed that most of the scattered shells composed of ridges and smooth cockle types. I also saw a curious assortment of lengthy green seaweed blades. It seemed almost as if someone had hacked away at their overgrown garden. Then, they had sprinkled the foliage over the ocean as an added condiment, leaving a spray of leftovers to float to shore.

However, before long I contemplated my mother's situation once more. She recently left the hospital after spending eight days there. A lung infection tightly gripped her body. Confined to a bed, she could not tend to herself. All movements, feeding, reaching for a drink, or going to the toilet required help. Wearing a diaper was a temporary solution while bedridden.

After my mother's condition improved, she resumed her stay at the residential care facility. I eagerly looked forward to speaking to her daily to check on her recovery. The entire situation grew quite unsettling because I only just returned from traveling overseas to visit her. Her sudden admission into hospital came as an unexpected turn of events. Especially since I had ensured she enjoyed a happy and memorable birthday celebration with relatives before my departure. On our last phone call, she mentioned her bottom was highly uncomfortable from sitting down all the time. The staff applied cream. The soreness stemmed from nappy rash.

I experienced a sense of powerlessness and sympathy for her. She was still weak and not 100% in health. No miracle paw-paw ointment was available to her.

I pondered the situation with every sandy step. Worry sank my footprints deeper. Then, like the flip of a switch, a thought suddenly popped into my head. A solution that might aid in soothing that specific sore spot for my mother. She should wear a sarong—a loose skirt fashioned from brightly coloured fabric worn wrapped around the body. This will cover her privates, allow her to ditch wearing underwear for a few days and give the area an airing. Warm confinement would only irritate and delay healing. I felt eager to phone her to tell her about my remedy. This revelation brought me hope. I couldn't be by her side, but I remained able to share words of comfort and encouragement.

At that moment, I observed two leafy green plant strands on the seashore right in front of me, near a motionless, transparent jellyfish. They were positioned precisely—one settled over the over as if purposely placed. The lengths of each blade differed. The image presented a cross. I instantly stopped in my tracks. It was a sign, literally. A private message for my witness only.

My desperate thoughts floated out on a veil of salty spritz to sail the ocean breeze. The symbol acknowledged me, my pondering, my predicament. It rested just a footstep away from my bare toes. I might have easily missed it. Awash with amazement at the sudden vision, I took my mobile phone and captured the sight immediately.

No sooner had I snapped to save the remarkable occurrence onto my camera roll, when a wave lapped into shore and whisked away the holy symbol. This was a gift. For my eyes to see and my mind to hold. I had a deep perception of being blessed, and in that moment, I felt comforted and reassured. It instilled faith and served as a reminder. Even through uncertain times, I was not alone, and neither was my mother.

A Sign (16.9.23)

Rehab

JOHN HUGHES

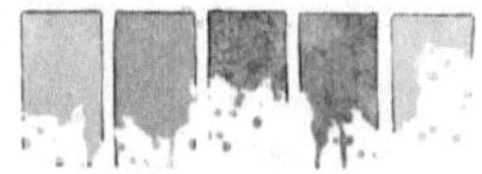

Desperate, Distressed, Weary: these words caught my eye as I scanned the Sherwood Cliffs Rehab Centre newsletter. Situated near Coffs Harbour on the mid-NSW coast, this facility has brought hope and restoration to many broken lives for over 35 years. A front-page report drew attention to the young men in Australia facing serious life challenges. Often emerging from broken families, many men struggle to hold secure work and relationships. Despite living in the 'lucky country', our alienated environment can often lead to a murky mix of destructive choices, of drug and alcohol misuse, mental health decline and despair.

I had been scanning the newsletter on and off when time permitted, and late in the day I made the call, and agreed to see an extra patient, a 'squeeze-in'. Our conversation started with those words: 'I feel like killing myself.'

In reality, it was the end of an exhausting day at work. Internally, I questioned my own judgment in consenting to this now-fraught consultation time. George had only been out of jail for a few days. He was unexpectedly well-dressed and clean-shaven, but desperate. Tears welled and his voice started to choke as he tried to hold back the emotional floodgates. A month before, I had been asked to provide his medical details to a local watchhouse. Release was conditional on entering a drug rehab centre and his primary need today was to obtain a referral.

Our practice had come in contact with George during the COVID-19 challenges of 2020. Even then, he'd came across as a frustrated, angry man not coping with neck pain. He had ruptured a disc in his cervical spine in 2010 and had chosen to misuse alcohol and prescription drugs to push on with his pain.

I'd describe George as driven. Modern capitalism offers our world the toxic mixture of hope for a good life and the slavish necessity to work hard to reach our dreams. George wanted to 'set up' his two bright young daughters with a good education. With the COVID pandemic changes, he adapted quickly to the new telehealth option for healthcare. His contact was often made in a crisis. These phone consultations were mostly unsatisfactory. George began to specialise in last-minute calls. A regular reason for them was work. He was often leaving on a six-week fishing trip the next day, and needed scripts to cover him while at sea.

His bright, nimble intelligence allowed him to successfully achieve a maritime skipper's licence. He had excelled in this role, and was sought after by employers. Alcohol has long been synonymous with the life of a sailor. George had consumed his fair share of grog and drugs in this industry, but now he was working for a good boss who ran a 'fleet of dry boats'. This boss had become a friend—someone who believed in George. There was good money to be made fishing and George embraced his new work opportunity.

Sadly, George also now needed money for more than a good family future. He was becoming dependent on both alcohol and prescription medication. Expenses were on the up and up. Phone calls, doctor's visits, pharmacy bills were all climbing over and trampling his dreams. Telehealth offered some respite as these consultations were initially designated as 'bulk-billed' only. At times, George felt so pressured that he simply yelled down the phone.

I kept a professional calm, and carefully worked toward a respectful relationship. I have encountered more than a few 'Georges' in my time. It wasn't rocket science to expect to find an isolated, lonely, desperate person behind the veneer of bluster and aggression. We were now more genuinely present to each other, and George began to share his story.

Christians find ourselves in God's story. This helps us deal with life and death. A core component of this story is that our lives are a gift from God, and life essentially takes the form of a journey back to God.

George's partner of eight years—the mother of his girls—had tragically been overwhelmed by her own desperation and trauma. She had suicided at the beginning of the COVID-19 pandemic. Illicit substances had not saved her soul and she had snuffed out her own life. George was locked down in grief. He was pacing his own cage.

Chronic despair is the plight of many indigenous people, both globally and in Australia. In our country, these people face very high rates of incarceration, poor socioeconomic and chronic health issues. The good clothes and clean-cut image belied such a heritage. Racial and cultural pressures for indigenous people are very hard to push through. At their best, organic cultures are uncomplicatedly family-orientated. Family is always family and in these tragic circumstances, George's mum became the loving stability that his girls needed.

George also shared he had fathered an older daughter to another woman. It was during a reckless youth phase. He confessed he'd treated this woman badly. George showed a glimpse of pride as he spoke of seeing that his eldest daughter was doing well through Facebook posts. Despite being completely cut off from her, George was man enough to admit her mother had done a great job at parenting.

I sometimes describe my role in primary care medicine as being a 'pain junkie.' Around 80% of primary health care encounters include an emotional or mental wellbeing component. There is a touch of isolation, desperation, and brokenness in all of us. From the first time George yelled at me on the phone, I was in. Here was a human being writhing in suffering and despair. He was manipulative to boot.

For an experienced doctor, this level of alienation, the reaping of the rewards of a God-forsaking life, is heavy going. But it is not necessarily hopeless. To a follower of Jesus, someone like George elicits a compassionate, self-giving response. After all, both Jesus and George share the cry, 'My God, my God, why have You given up on me?'

I was getting to know George better with every contact. His distress had its beginnings in the abusive attentions of a neighbour when he was a child. George describes his own family group as good. Unfortunately, however, their home was encircled by evil. Sexual abuse is always destructive to children. Here was the kind of neighbourly attention that crushes the human spirit. This is the anti-community that never raises healthy children.

From his compromised start, and despite wholehearted family love, George struggled with developmental transitions. In his own words, his adolescence was reckless. He learnt to misuse alcohol and illicit drugs. His angry frustration overflowed to violence and disrespect for others. In all of this, he was fortunate enough to have sufficient good mentors to productively guide his natural intelligence. Becoming a fishing boat skipper has been an opportunity to thrive despite inner turmoil.

Nothing had prepared George for finding the woman, the love of his life, hanging lifeless and defeated. All the pandemics of history were pale clouds in the distance to the final reality of death before him. He was simply not ready for this body blow. After the neighbourly abuse, he was always a little on edge, always distrusting—at times, paranoid.

As the misuse of alcohol and prescription medication escalated, a precarious path was opening up. Work performance moved off the sweet spot and George's boss was quick to notice. In an irrational act of 'biting the hand that feeds', an explosive argument erupted with his employer.

Providence is the general way God relieves suffering, the way that good emerges out of bad. Despite the conflict, George's employer assessed the context as a moment requiring leadership and grace. He arranged to pay the fee for a private alcohol rehab program. When people are open to the healing love of God, as opposed to selfish interest, genuine transformation is possible.

It was now past dinner time. Yet promptings from the Spirit were feeding into my mindful presence with this man. I couldn't rescue George from his despair—but was I willing walk a mile in his shoes? Was I willing to introduce him to Jesus, the centre of my own life? I began to prepare the referral required for the rehab centre. Time seemed both limited and pressured.

The dancing, life-giving Spirit of God provided the right moment. Perhaps my empathetic curiosity for George's life story opened the door. Quite unexpectedly, this dead man walking asked, 'Are you a Christian, doc?'

The professional restraint that encases the life of a Christian doctor was cracked open. The role of doctor in a vulnerable health context is unquestionably powerful. Nietzsche's 'will to power' is handed on a platter to all who succeed in passing an MBBS exam. The appropriate honing of ethics and clinical skill allow a genuine space for human connection, but it is risky territory. It can be a 'risk' to decide to play God.

While I was writing my rehab referral, the possibility of introducing the Sherwood Cliffs newsletter had crossed my mind. George had been sent to jail because his obsessional jealousy would not let go of the thought that his new partner, who had accepted him and his bright-eyed girls without conditions, had cheated on him. His whole life of mistrust, built from the experience of sexual abuse, had made his vision of any relationship curved and twisted. Hurt dominated trust. During his first vicariously provided attempt at reform, he had gained much, but not enough to dislodge this vengeful flaw.

George fought his feelings. He had accepted short-term treatment to medicate this paranoia, but the pressure built. Unable to forgive himself, he could not surrender his jealousy. With a skin full of alcohol, he bashed and bashed his girlfriend. Everything within the home was assaulted. When the police arrived, he tried to battle with them.

During the COVID pandemic, we all became aware of rising rates of domestic violence. Instead of the expected patience of love, a litany of frustration, fear and unforgiven hurts have rushed into the safe haven of homes. Since wartime, women in our communities have faced the reality that their potential for violent death is most likely in their own home—at the hands of lovers.

There were tears in George's eyes again as he confessed his sin. This kind, gentle surrogate mother and lover was now battered and bruised. A woman drained of humanity. History was ready to repeat itself. George's mother, rock-like, now accepted complete responsibility for his girls. This is not such an uncommon reality in our world. The court rightfully excluded George from their care after the 'day of violence'. In the quietness of this moment, he added to his offences by admitting to a suspicion I myself had begun to hold. George had started misusing prescription drugs again in the wind-up to his crisis-induced incarceration. His own woundedness could not be contained.

I looked down at the Sherwood Cliff's newsletter on my desk. 'When our men first make contact with Sherwood, they are desperate, distressed, and weary from the (godless) drought in their life. Circumstances and choices that have seemingly, effortlessly drained their every reservoir have left them running on empty. The very essence of life is almost gone. Hope is fading and the future is uncertain.'

George was disqualified—appropriately—from any contact with his battered former partner or daughters and, after a month without liberty, he was sentenced to three months of rehabilitation at a prescribed facility. There were no other options.

My tired mind was swirling. Where would the wind of the Spirit take us now? I had confessed my allegiance to Christ.

The crack in the door that the Spirit had opened widened as I looked up from my keyboard and George said, 'You know, doc, I need a complete change inside. If I have got any chance, I need to start again.'

Bingo! I began telling the story I had heard of another indigenous male from Katherine in the Northern Territory. Katherine is a place of rare beauty. Tourists flock to visit and experience Kakadu. Each year, this town also hosts the Katherine Christian Convention, where aboriginal Christians gather with other sisters and brothers to worship, fellowship, and be exposed to Bible teaching and gospel transformation.

Katherine, then, was also a centre for alcohol purchase and distribution — grog that would regularly make its way to 'dry' communities. One of the aboriginal men in Katherine was a notorious alcoholic. His drinking and anti-social behaviour had unsettled more than one good tourist, Christian visitor and local resident. One day, all of a sudden, the gospel power of a living Christ gripped his life. His transformation was astonishing. I shared this story with George. It was a story of the hope he had articulated.

I sensed a permission to go on and conveyed to this broken man before me the way many healing stories in the gospels capture moments when people who are desperate cry out for help. The stories capture the power of God's love to heal, to restore and renew people's lives. I told him I wished we had the time and space to hear the stories together. The Spirit was connecting us together at this point. Time carried that sense of standing still.

I picked up the newsletter and showed him the story of the desperate, distressed, and weary men. It resonated and he asked for details of how to contact Sherwood Cliffs. God always knows us better than we can know ourselves. As he gazed at this 'praise letter,' he was able to reflect, 'I think three months won't be long enough. I should look into going there to get the job done.'

This Christian rehab was established in 1988. I had become aware of its possibilities and had made a few referrals over the years. As the story went, 'On arrival, the men welcome change and this new opportunity offers hope.' Many men are bitter and hardened by their brokenness. Surrender to a rehab helps to complete the detox process. Regaining dignity by working a farm without the distractions and temptations of drugs and alcohol is good. But George could also see this as a haven where a prodigal could return to the home of God's love, in Jesus.

For now, I undertook to photocopy the Sherwood Cliffs contact details for George, and then set to work to finish the referral. He respected the time constraints and went back to the waiting room. I printed up the collaborative information which would help those involved in the official rehab process, finalised my letter, and then photocopied the promised details.

When I looked up, I found George reading a Bible placed in the waiting room. Not many people stop to enter into God's story of creation, sin, salvation, and future hope. A nudge from the Spirit had timed it right for George. 'Hey, doc, here is the story of a desperate woman who touches Jesus and is healed.'

Our previous conversation was enough introduction to the story—God's story of grace was now speaking with George. As I gave him the paperwork, I made an offer for him to keep the Bible. I could see a smile. He took the referral, the Bible, and made for the door with a bounce in his step. I wished him well.

We had progressed so far in a short time. Should I have pressed on and introduced this man to the lover of our souls? Maybe it's the professional context. Maybe it's the unforced rhythms of grace. In the openness of this end to my day, I felt joy. There is no better word.

An article in the newsletter, so central to our conversation, took up the image of soaking rain as the felt experience of the men who make it to Sherwood Cliffs. To such broken men, they make this offer: 'Allow the rain to soak deep into your life! Be open to God and allow Him to nourish you, refresh you, and restore you. Be open to God and allow Him to guide you, to refocus your perspective and your life. Be open to God and allow Him to teach you, to rebuild that which was broken.'

So, why not?

Immanuel in the Mundane

PAMELA JULIAN

'*A-gain,*' our three-year-old pleaded.

So I read *Monty Frog* for the tenth or eleventh time that evening.

'A-*gain!*'

'A-*gain!*'

By now he could look at the pictures and I could recite the entire book almost from memory.

'A-*gain!*' was his catchcry for anything he loved and wanted to have over and over. It didn't matter if it was a story, or a game or a song, 'A-*gain!*' he would say, and we would comply.

Sometimes it was boring, singing the same little ditty, or pushing the toy cars along the same road. But our son never tired of it. He got excited in preparation for what he knew was going to happen next. Children love familiarity; they love the anticipation of something predictable happening over and over again.

I think it gives them a sense of security; it shows them something of the natural laws of our planet. The writing on each page of this book will always say the same thing; the car will always roll down the slope; the song always ends with clapping.

For us it can become tedious, because we have already learnt these laws. Sometimes I would include interesting variations to provide myself with some relief from the monotony. This might work and he would laugh—children also enjoy the unexpected and ridiculous.

But sometimes he would correct me. 'Tell it right,' he would say. He even got quite upset once or twice because he wanted it 'told right'.

As women, wives and mothers, we so often spend much of our time doing the mundane. Folding clothes, washing, cooking, and tidying up. It can be very predictable, boring even. Sometimes we change the routine to add a little spice—go shopping *before* we tidy the house; change washing day to Tuesday. Don't get me wrong—I loved being a mother. I also love variety in my life. But some days I struggled with the routine of housework, the repetitiveness of playing with a small child. The days could drag. I longed for outings, visits and entertainment.

Yet the time spent in housework, the intensity of one-on-one with a small child, has its rewards in a job well done.

I sometimes wonder if God gets bored with the mundaneness of running the universe. I mean, He could do *anything* He likes—build another one, zoom around outer space, go away somewhere *quiet*. Yet He doesn't. He made a commitment to us. He chooses to sustain the universe as we know it with its natural laws and constancy. The sun rises each day; gravity keeps our feet on the ground; rain and snow fall at His command.

There is nothing half-hearted in His work in the universe—there is no 'I can't be bothered with this today.' He doesn't leave. The Bible tells us that He is involved fully in every aspect of it—always working to bring about His purposes.

Our Heavenly Father is interested in all the little unexciting things in our lives. He protects and cares for us in our day-to-day needs; patiently listens to our repeated requests, our whinges; He provides our daily bread. Gives us little surprises. Sounds rather like a mother's day, doesn't it?

Our lives may not feel exciting as home-makers, but perhaps we see the inside of God's loyalty and faithfulness to His creation in this role more than in any other. He's here with us—Immanuel, *God with us*—in the mundane.

Romans 12:1 MSG

> *So here's what I want you to do, God helping you: Take your everyday, ordinary life—your sleeping, eating, going-to-work, and walking around life—and place it before God as an offering.*

Chasing God

JO WANMER

Hunger. That gnawing, unsatisfied feeling. Not the vacuum that fills with a good steak. The emptiness that cries out for more of God. David likened it to thirst, like the deer's need for water. Only God satisfies my soul and I was stuck in a desert again. Dry.

A revival at Lakeland, Florida, sparking amazing miracles, filled our news. The meetings flowed into our church via livestream. Late at night we watched from across the world, we joined the singing and dancing, listened to every word. But it stirred my hunger, rather than satisfied it. I wanted more. One of the songs spoke to me. 'I've been past this place so many times, but this time I'm going in.'

Going there was a pipe-dream. This event was on the other side of the world. Impossible.

Then I realised my mother's inheritance was coming. It wasn't much… but enough to fly to the USA. Once the idea was birthed it grew wings. Within a week, I found myself enroute to Tampa, Florida, with Noel and Margaret as companions. Six nights of accommodation were booked before our return flights. Literally a flying trip. Chasing more of God.

Noel knew America, so we followed his lead. He asked for my licence when he hired the car. I objected, explaining I'd never before driven on the wrong side of the road. He waved my fears away. He needed me to drive home from the meetings because he would be drunk… drunk on the Holy Spirit. What about me? Hadn't I flown for endless hours to be overwhelmed myself?

The massive tent held eight thousand people. By arriving two hours before the meetings started, we could soak through worship practice, giving us bonus hours. Noel registered us as pastors, gaining us access to extra training. Every afternoon we waited in the 'International Visitors' line for the doors to open. We raced to get good seats and then claimed a spot in the mosh pit. We sang for three hours and then joined in the prayers and the messages. Five hours later we left—Noel often so overcome by the Spirit that he could barely walk to the car. I drove, feeling like a designated driver, the one who never got drunk. Nights passed and I felt no nearer to God than when I'd left home.

'God… why don't you touch me? I've paid all Mum's money. Why do you touch Noel and not me?'

In the huge tent I could scream at God and no one noticed. Everyone was yelling in worship and praise. *Was I the only one in eight thousand struggling to connect? Was I the only one God was ignoring?*

As we drove back to our hotel, and I concentrated on driving on the right, Noel related his amazing experiences with God. And then: 'What did God say to you, Jo?'

On the fourth night, I had an answer. 'God told me I was lukewarm.'

Noel stopped talking, eyes wide. 'You're not lukewarm!'

I exploded. 'It's the only thing God's said to me. It's better than nothing.'

This correction was shocking, but it beat silence. The passage from Revelation was familiar. I didn't like it but I knew it. 'You're shameful, poor and blind, and you are clueless about it.'

The next day was busy as usual. Shop here, hear someone speak there, back to the hotel for a quick rest. We'd leave for dinner by three to get to revival by four… come home at about eleven or twelve and fall into bed.

That night I felt expectant. Surely God would say more. I had read the passage until I knew it by heart. I had made a choice. I could have ignored the thought, passed it off as my imagination. But I chose to take it as my word from God and act on it. I arrived that night with a plan. It started with repentance. In the melee of the mosh pit that night, I repented for being lukewarm. For being blind. For being poor in spirit. The passage advised me to buy gold, refined in the fire, white clothes to cover my nakedness and salve for my eyes. How could I buy anything from the Almighty God? I had nothing to spend. How could I follow His instruction? Sobbing, in my desperate need to touch God's heart, I gave Him everything. It wasn't much in a worldly sense but it was all I had.

'God, I give You our house, our cars, our business. There's not much money but it's Yours. I give You my husband, my children, my grandchildren. My life is Yours.'

When everything I could think of was laid down, given to Him, I heard God's whisper and it overwhelmed me. Not the sound, or the intensity but the hugeness of what He asked.

DON'T GO HOME YET. STAY HERE LONGER

'But, God. I have to get back to the business.'

I THOUGHT YOU GAVE THAT TO ME

'But, Steve needs me.'

YOU GAVE HIM TO ME, TOO. TRUST ME

'We don't have enough money.'

YOU EVEN GAVE THAT TO ME

I had no excuse. God had accepted my miserly offerings. It seemed it was enough. And He was taking charge of my life.

But what if I hadn't heard Him? How could I possibly stay? I wrestled throughout the meeting.

We drove back to the hotel with Noel laughing and praising God. He'd had heavenly visions and been taken up to heaven.

He was overcome by the wonder of God. I was overwhelmed by the request of God.

'God asked me to stay longer.' I could barely hear my own voice over the laughter, which stilled.

'What did you say?'

'God has asked me to stay longer, to not go home yet.'

Noel turned and stared at me. 'What are you going to do?'

'I'll sleep on it and talk to Steve tomorrow.'

'But tomorrow is our last night… we fly out at six the next morning.'

What could Steve say when I told him God had asked me to stay? He asked how long but I didn't know. The decision was made. I would stay in Florida by myself. I wasn't worried about that. I was an independent, self-sufficient woman. But how would they cope at home, without me? The difficulties started with changing the tickets. Every change cost money we didn't have. And with every phone call, the machines couldn't decipher my Australian accent.

By the time I left for the last meeting with my friends, the flights were changed. No turning back. The next morning, we would leave at 4 am. They would go to the airport. I would hire a smaller car and return to Lakeland.

It was midnight when Noel knocked on the door to our room. 'We have a problem. I've just been down to reception. There are no vacancies here. We have to find you another hotel.'

My heart dropped. I hadn't packed as I wasn't leaving. And where would I go? Right now, we needed to go to bed.

'It's fine.' I waved Noel's concern away. 'I'll find something after you leave.'

He'd made the decision I would only stay one extra week. I'd appreciated his leadership. Now he refused to leave the country until he'd found some suitable hotel for me. The city was overbooked. After much online searching we found a place. He wasn't really comfortable about it, but I booked it and crawled into bed at 2 am. Huddled under the blankets so I wouldn't wake my roommate, I skyped Steve. Reality was suffocating me. He needed to move money in the hope our finances wouldn't implode. This was crazy. Had I really heard God? I curled up in a ball and tried to summon faith… that substance of things hoped for. What had I done?

Noel drove to Tampa. We were all over-tired. As they grabbed their bags and raced to catch the plane, loneliness engulfed me. Just me and God. Suddenly I felt very small. I rented another car. Worried about cash, I didn't pay for a GPS. I knew my way around now. I didn't need help.

To return to Lakeland, I needed to use the freeway. It had a toll booth requiring a coin. I had none. I assured Noel it was okay. I'd just stop and buy something.

Leaving the car rental garage, I eased into the traffic, my heart thumping, driving on the right. I needed a shop that was open early. I couldn't go back any other way. I had no map. This was the only route I knew. Head aching, palms sweating, I eventually pulled in at a bakery. I made my request and the lady shook her head and turned away. What had I done?

She didn't understand English, let alone Australian. I'd stopped in a Spanish area. I tried again. God rescued me by sending another customer who rolled her eyes and translated my request.

Eyes stinging, body stiff from stressful driving, I found my way back to the old hotel. Ignoring the pull of my bed, I shoved everything in the car and went looking for my new hotel, where I could sleep. Using a basic map picked up from the hotel foyer, I navigated across town and found the correct street. My shoulders and fingers were taut, aching. I tried to relax. I was on the road. All I had to do was find number 1,546. Easy. Numbers flashed past, but there was no motel. I passed where the number should have been, turned around and came back. Either I was crazy or it wasn't there. Maybe I was crazy.

Parking in a shopping centre car park, I reviewed my map. I considered myself good with maps, but on the other side of the globe everything seemed upside down. Swallowing my tears, I strengthened myself. My bed which was paid for, had to be just down there. Determined, I pulled out of the carpark. But I forgot. I did the Aussie thing and checked the traffic to the left, not the right. When I looked up, a car was filling my windscreen. There was no way to avoid it. There was no time to brake. Yelling 'Jesus', I closed my eyes and expected to die.

Nothing happened. When I opened my eyes, the car had disappeared. My car was driving on the road. There was no way I could have a missed that car… except for angelic intervention. Shaking I found a place to stop. Thankful but broken. Superwoman was undone.

Head on the steering wheel, I wept. Rescued by a God whom I treated shabbily at best. My trust was in me and my ability… not in God. There real repentance erupted, not in a big tent, surrounded by thousands, but beside the road, alone, broken with traffic whooshing past.

God, please get me to the motel.

Driving the same road in the same direction for the umpteenth time was not helping. I parked, humbled myself and walked into a car yard to request help. The lady could understand me and explained their streets have a north arm and a south arm. I was on the south arm and I needed the northern one. I headed north and found the motel. I couldn't see the entry but confident, I took the road that went in front of it. But it bypassed my bed and took me straight onto the freeway. Once again, swept along by fast traffic, I drove south!

Two hours before I needed to leave for the night meeting, I fell into my room. It was a cheap motel in a shady looking area. To access my car I needed to walk the exterior passage, descend the stairs and walk around the building. No security guard here. I pushed down fear and I decided to skype Steve. But the internet wouldn't connect. I rang reception who told me they'd look at it in the morning.

At least I'd thought to buy drinking water. I grabbed one of the bottles but my fingers weren't strong enough to break the seal. Sobbing, I fell asleep.

I woke disoriented, feeling drained by exhaustion. However it was time to face the streets and go to the revival. I could skip this meeting… rest tonight… try again tomorrow. But I'd spent all this money. I needed to attend. I pulled myself to the shower.

My arrival, later than usual, meant a long walk from the car park. Every other night we had found other Aussies to sit with… but this night everyone spoke another language. I found myself a chair and sat alone. The revival pulsated around me. Miracles were happening but, to me, God seemed silent. Maybe I couldn't hear. I felt completely stripped, naked.

On leaving the car park, I searched for the entry to the freeway. A new hotel meant a different road. I turned down a ramp. In front of me was one of those big red signs. WRONG WAY. GO BACK.

My heart pounded. I broke into a sweat. How does one go back? And where to? I spun the wheel and bumped the car onto a grassy island. No other car would crash into me there while I got my bearings.

Father, I can't do anything. Indeed, I'm poor, pitiful and blind. Please help me.

I bumped the car back onto a road heading the correct direction. Somehow, I found the motel and fell into bed, unable to even tell Steve I was okay—alive only by God's miraculous intervention. The next morning, I fronted the service desk, sobbing. I explained I had to be able to connect to home. The woman raised her eyebrows, sighed and told me to ring this number and organise someone to fix the problem. One more hurdle to overcome with my accent.

The other two would be nearly home. I longed to be with them. Yet… I had given everything to God, including home.

Lord, You counselled me to buy gold refined in the fire, white clothes to cover my nakedness, and salve for my eyes so I can see. I see now my self-sufficiency, my pride, wanting to do it myself in my way. I'm in the fire. I feel naked, embarrassed, alone. Help me.

Someone fixed the internet. I attacked the water bottles with a blunt knife, opening a few for later. I connected with Steve and rested a little. I grabbed some things from a supermarket and returned to the big tent. Joining the other pastors, feeling like a fraud, I sat under good teaching and at the communion table. The Spirit strengthened me.

Worship began, the mosh pit pulsated, hands waved in the air, bodies jumped and danced. At the back I worshipped God my way in the quieter environment, comfortable in His presence. That night I reached home without any drama. Every time I went to my car to drive I opened what I thought was the driver's door, only to discover no steering wheel.

It appeared I could do nothing right. My need for God increased.

Was God talking? Yes… as a companion, a friend, a guide, the way He'd always communicated to me. My despair reduced each day as I realised I didn't need what others had. I needed the unique touch the Lord had for me.

The fourth night I went to the counsellor's training, saving a seat near the front for the message. In the meeting I saw a man struggling to get out of a wheelchair. I stood beside him, hoping a real counsellor would come. He was large man, towering over me. With absolute determination he began to walk the five metres to the rail at the stage. I stood with him, speaking strength into his legs every time they weakened. He would straighten again and one shuffle after another he pushed forward. From the stage, they were yelling out words of knowledge—ears are being opened, God is touching grief, healing lungs. I listened to each word, waiting, hoping for a word of healing for this man with MS.

'Now there are dental miracles. If you need a dental miracle, open your mouth.' For over a year I'd been asking God to heal one of my teeth. I opened my mouth, but the man's legs gave way. I yelled, 'Strength to those legs.' He straightened. The moment had passed. Later on, I helped him back to his wheelchair, still praying for his total healing. His demonstrated faith inspired me.

The next morning, I was talking to Steve on my computer, when I saw a flash of gold. I opened my mouth and peered into the mirror. One of my teeth was gold—gleaming, shining gold! I screamed. Further searching uncovered a second one, right at the back. Steve demanded an explanation.

'Gold teeth… God has given me gold teeth.'

Gold! In my bumbling way, I'd followed His word and somehow bought gold. I raced down stairs to the dining room and told everyone who would listen.

That night a row of people with familiar accents sat beside me. Aussies. How exciting. I showed them my teeth. One lady squeezed in beside me, desperate to get gold teeth too. The next night her mouth was like a Christmas tree. Every filling in her mouth had been turned to gold.

When I left the tent for the last time, it was a strange feeling. No one to farewell. Just me, alone, walking to my car. But not alone. My relationship with God was now in a deeper place. My hunger had been self-inflicted; my proud self-sufficiency had been choking my relationship with God and blocking the spiritual food I craved.

I had been refined in the fire and was taking home gold.

Fifteen years later I still have gleaming, shiny gold teeth… gifts from my Father. And I know He is always with me. His sufficiency is more reliable than mine.

The Goldfish and the Rock

LYNDA HAMMOND

'For I am about to do something new. See, I have already begun!
Do you not see it? I will make a pathway through the wilderness.
I will create rivers in the dry wasteland.'

Isaiah 43:19 NLT

As I looked out at our backyard, I had an ominous feeling in the pit of my stomach. The house that we were renting needed significant plumbing work. The only good news was that we didn't have to pay for it!

The plumbers were in, their heads just showing above the deep channels they had dug in our backyard. As I looked at our unrecognisable backyard—I KNEW it was speaking about changes that had a lot more meaning than just a new set of pipes!

Life was sweet. You could say I was in a 'purple patch'—living the dream as I ran our local Church Bible College Hub. When I wasn't doing that, I was at home, available to Jeff and the kids, or in my 'home office' studying or praying. My 'home office' was the garden shed I had adapted.

I loved it.

It was my personal sanctuary. It was where I did lecture and sermon prep. And now I couldn't even get there!

It wasn't just the ministry work that I enjoyed. I had (apart from volunteer work) been a 'stay-at-home' mum for the last twenty years. My world had been relatively uncomplicated and safe. I like being home. I like being emotionally and mentally present to my family. I enjoy baking and reading and, well—just being home!

Back to the plumbers' handiwork in our garden. I was right; it was prophetic. At that time, change at many levels was about to occur in my life. We had to leave our lovely home as the owners wanted to do some renovating and sell it—no more garden office!

I also knew it was time to look for paid work outside the home. There was a reason why that was not what I wanted to do. It was because home and church were my comfort zones. I was afraid to 'get out there'.

Apart from needing the money my job would bring in, I knew the Lord wanted to 'update' and 'upskill' me. I also knew it was only for a season. Of these two things, I was sure. Even though I was nervous, I was excited about what this would mean.

While moving, we had to empty our fishpond and find a new home for the fish. Their new home would be at a friend's place in their unused swimming pool. The young man came to get the fish and managed to net all bar one. It was the biggest fish. That fish dodged the net in every way it could. It would hide under rocks and take quick escapes. We knew it would die if we didn't catch it, as the water was draining away quickly!

As I watched that goldfish, it reminded me of myself. The Lord was trying to move me into another place but, inside my soul, I wanted to dodge this considerable change. I couldn't help but smile at myself. I knew the Lord was painting me a very accurate picture, and along with that picture, letting me know He understood how I was feeling.

I felt comforted.

I applied for work in the local Medical Practice as a receptionist. In addition to moving house, I was also planning my daughter's wedding. It wasn't a brilliant mix. The day I went for the interview was a story in itself!

I got the job which, although highly challenging with a very steep learning curve, was a perfect fit. I loved the people contact, and there was a great sense of 'team' amongst the staff.

I was right. Some 'updating' and upskilling did take place, but it was only for a season. I was there for two years and am now running our local Bible College again.

What am I saying in all this? Somewhere in your journey, you may be tipped out of your comfort zone. Actually, there is a solid possibility you will. You may even be facing a similar scenario right now.

I want to encourage you that it will be ok. Even though that season was a massive stretch, I would not have missed it for anything.

One day, just before I was due to go to work, I was watching part of a movie, *Facing the Giants*. It was being previewed on a talk show just before its release. The scene they showed was when one of the players in the training session was blindfolded and had extra weight put on his back. With this excess weight, he had to get to the goalpost, not knowing how far away the finish line was.

That was precisely how I felt: carrying weight I thought I couldn't possibly hold and not knowing where the goalpost was. I genuinely did not feel I could pull this season off. Of course, the player got to the goalpost, and a huge lesson was learned. I was so encouraged. The Lord allowed that to be on the TV when I needed it!

I knew I would make it to my goalpost, even though I couldn't see it at that point.

The time comes when you must step into a different and challenging season. Maybe it's right now for you. Let me encourage you—you will make it. And when you have stepped into it, you will find strength and abilities within you that you never knew you had. You will come out of it enriched, trained, and with a greater capacity to carry the responsibilities God has for you.

Just like that goldfish who, at the end of that terrifying day, found himself in a much broader place, you will be so glad you came out from under the rock and said, 'Here I am, Lord—do what You will with me.'

Cheating Death

HAZEL BARKER

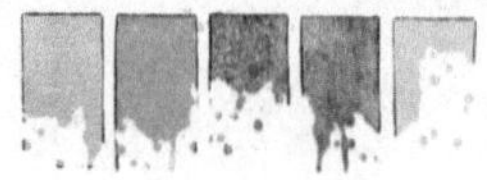

In 1941, when I was four, Japanese forces occupied Burma. Three years later, Britain commenced retaking the country and, to escape the bombing, our family sought refuge in a jungle village not far from the fabled city of Mandalay. Life was different from those memorably glorious days before the war when Dad had worked in the High Court of Rangoon. We had lived in a beautifully appointed home.

We stayed in a hut during the Japanese occupation. For fear of their troops, I remained indoors with Mum, together with my older sister, June, my little sister, Rose, and my young brother, Herman, who suffered from infantile paralysis. My father and two of my brothers, Rupert and Bertie, explored the jungle surrounding us. Food was scarce, and we suffered from diarrhoea and beri-beri.

By early 1945, British and Indian forces had fought their way back through northern Burma from the west, via the Ledo Road. From the east, American and Chinese forces entered Burma via the Stilwell Road. Each day brought swiftly changing news and rumours. Allied aircraft dropped pamphlets telling us of their mounting offensive while Japanese-controlled newspapers claimed to have shot down several planes and decimated Britain's 17th Division. Our fear and frustration escalated.

One morning after breakfast, Dad retired to the front room to read the news. Mum and I were clearing away the dishes in the kitchen when a thunderous knocking startled us. Dad slapped the newspaper down and rose to answer the door. I dropped the rag which served as a tea towel and hurried after him. The village headman stood there, accompanied by a soldier from the Burma Independence Army. With arms akimbo, the official barked out an order in Burmese, then pivoted on his heels and marched off.

The bamboo floor squeaked as Dad paced the room. After a few minutes, he came into the kitchen. 'The headman has ordered that a male representative from each household must report to his office at six sharp tomorrow morning.' He left us and continued pacing outside.

After the conquest of Burma, Japan had set up a military government to replace the civil one. They introduced a system of corvée requiring each household to supply unpaid labour to the government in lieu of income tax.

June leaned towards Mum. 'What'll Daddy do?'

'I don't know. If your father sends Rupert, he may be kept as a labourer, and we will never see him again.'

'But why? Daddy's stronger,' June said. 'Why won't Daddy go himself?'

'But he has to look after us.' Mum steadied herself against a wooden crate which served as a table. 'Who'll take care of us if he dies? His relatives will turn us out of this hut. Where will we live then?'

June put her arms around Mum. 'Rupert's the oldest, but Daddy will not be parted from him. He's his favourite.'

Mum sobbed. 'Sending Bertie would be worse. He's younger than Rupert and not as strong. He won't survive.'

Dad came back. He scowled at us.

'Who's to go, then?' Mum asked.

He spat out his answer. 'Rupert. Rupert will go.'

My mouth grew dry at the thought of losing my brother. A shudder passed through me, and I wanted to cry. At the same time, I was glad he wasn't sending Bertie, who was my favourite brother.

'Who else could I delegate?' Dad asked, as if in reply to my thoughts. 'Do I even have a choice? I can't afford to pay someone to take my place. I'll tell Rupert that, as the oldest son, it's his duty to represent the household.'

He had never explained his actions before, so I was surprised and puzzled. Only in later years, did I fully appreciate the anguish my parents suffered at the time.

The next morning, Rupert reported for duty as ordered. All I could do was to pray and agonise over his impending doom. Tired but excited, Rupert returned to us early next morning, when Dad was out for his usual walk. Joy overwhelmed me, and I thanked the Lord for my brother's safe return.

Mum hugged Rupert. 'We had no idea where you were taken. I could not sleep the whole night and kept praying for you.'

'We didn't go far. We were driven by trucks to a railway siding not far from here. They promised to let us go home once we'd done the job, but I didn't believe them. My friend, Owen, was there too, so I spoke to him about trying to escape, but he trusted them.'

Bertie shook his head. 'You'd have been tortured, if caught escaping.'

'We are not prisoners-of-war, so they were not too vigilant in guarding us. Besides, there were only two guards. I knew the risk of being captured and imagined water torture, or having my fingernails torn out, or being burned by cigarette butts, but it was a risk worth taking.' He shrugged and raised his arms, as though there had been no alternative.

I clenched my teeth so much they hurt. I knew Rupert was brave. He would never let out a whimper whenever Dad thrashed him, but facing death and torture was another thing. Rupert slumped into a seat; his hands clasped together. 'I tricked them and slipped boxes of cartridges into the water each time I crossed the stream.' Amazed at his audacity, I relished every word, visualising the scene.

Rupert's eyes shone as he spoke. 'I was assigned to a group to carry arms and ammunition from lorries to railway wagons. The wagons stood at a siding over a kilometre from the station, tucked away beneath a canopy of trees that hid them from allied planes. Perspiration poured down our bodies as we unloaded the cargo from the trucks and crossed a stream in the hot sun. When we paused to drink, soldiers hit us with their rifle butts and moved us on. I staggered under my load, carrying as much as I could, hoping to please the Japanese guards. I stumbled along with cartridge boxes, discreetly slipping some into the stream. I did the same each time I returned with a new load. I worked hard until darkness pressed in, and we were ordered to stop work.'

Rupert took a breath. 'After a meal of stewed vegetables and rice, a guard leapt on one of the cartridge crates. "You'll be sent home at daybreak once you've unloaded the wagons. Now sleep." Two soldiers stood guard, smoking. After some time, a sentry stubbed out his cigarette and wandered off, humming a popular Japanese song. Only one remained. I crawled away from my sleeping companions. A twig snapped. I lay motionless, scarcely daring to breathe. The soldier had finished his cigarette and was looking at his fingernails, so I lowered my head and continued to crawl. A sharp thorn pierced my hand. I suppressed a cry of pain, and lay still, gathering strength before crawling off like a soldier I'd seen in a movie. Once out of sight, I leapt to my feet and raced home. It was a moonlight night, and I feared a bombing raid. Once I got clear of the camp, I ran and ran. My breath was ragged, and I was so thirsty, but all I could think of was freedom. The soldiers wouldn't miss me, and Owen would certainly not split on me. I realised that once home, I'd be safe. I was more afraid of meeting a tiger, so I broke off a branch from a tree to protect myself.'

I shivered and hugged myself with fear as Rupert continued his story. 'I kept thinking an enemy lurked in every shadow. The jungle sounds eerie at night with jackals howling and monkeys chattering. But I hoped a tiger would go for them — not me.' Rupert grinned. I realised he was proud to have gone in place of Dad. Proud to risk his life for us. Proud to have sabotaged the enemy.

When Dad returned, his eyes opened wide to see Rupert. 'We must hide you. What if a search party comes looking for you?'

'They won't miss me. We were too many of us to count. They just piled us into trucks and drove off into the jungle. I've explored the area around the village whenever I finished my chores and know the jungle paths like the back of my hand. When I ran off from the camp, I made sure I wasn't followed, and took a roundabout route home.'

Dad's huge sigh told us a load had dropped from his shoulders.

Rupert was fortunate to have escaped that night. The rest of the group never returned. They were dragged off to forced-labour camps, where they toiled on the Thai–Burma railway along with prisoners-of-war. The construction took seventeen months to complete and around one hundred and fifty thousand forced labourers lost their lives on the Death Railway. Rupert's friend, Owen, was one of them.

When he was first taken away, his family mourned and prayed for his return. After the war, his younger brother travelled to Thailand, hoping to gain some news of his missing brother. There, a native described to him the fate of one of the prisoners—a young Anglo-Indian boy who had died and was buried in the camp. It could have been Owen. Had my brother not escaped, he would probably have died there too.

Perhaps because he had wandered into the jungle so frequently and been bitten by mosquitoes, Rupert contracted malaria towards the end of hostilities. He lay shivering in bed with his blanket pulled over his head even on the hottest days. After he perspired, the fever disappeared, leaving him weak and listless. Within a short time, the cycle would repeat itself, completely sapping his strength.

We'd long run out of quinine, so Dad called a herbalist who prescribed neem tea and ordered Rupert to remain in bed. It is imperative for a patient with malaria to rest. Neem trees grew in profusion at the village. We picked the leaves and boiled them as instructed. Rupert drank cups of the herbal profusion without complaining. The bitter concoction broke his fever but the cycle recommenced within a few weeks.

By the end of 1944, it seemed death was about to place its hand on Rupert's shoulder and claim him. My sister, June, had already been carried off by plague in March that year. It was too much to bear. I fretted for her and feared for Rupert.

Allied forces were, however, almost at the gates of Mandalay, ready to re-take the city. When the sun sank beneath the horizon and spread a dark mantle over the village, the sound of shells and the roar of trucks repeatedly broke the stillness of the night. Convoys, like one continuous caterpillar humping up and down the Burma Road, trucked Japanese reinforcements to the northern frontline and returned with casualties to hospitals in Mandalay. One night I heard explosions just over the hill. My heart hammered in rhythm with the pounding of guns.

Day by day the thunder of twenty-pounders grew closer and louder. Allied forces crossed the river just south of Mandalay and, cutting off all road access towards the city, they commenced a barrage of shelling. Explosives roared and trucks rolled past. Life in the village simply carried on.

February slid into the hot days of March. One sweltering day, Rupert lay in bed shivering, a blanket covering his head. Mum sat beside him, weak and famished. Dad was out. Bertie, Rose and I paced listlessly between the stilts under the hut. Bertie gazed into the distance, his head to one side, as though he were trying to listen.

An uplifting sound echoed across the plains. We remembered it from every New Year's Day celebration that had occurred in those wonderful days before the war. The skirl of bagpipes stirred the very core of my soul. Even now, I can shut my eyes and call to mind that sublime moment. My pulse raced and, by the way my little sister tightened her grip on my hand, I knew she was afraid. The sound was strange to her ears.

'It's the British!' Bertie streaked off, swift as an arrow, in the direction of the main road.

'Come on, Rose.' I held my sister's hand and raced after him.

We rushed towards the call of the bagpipes, drawn like pieces of iron to a magnet. Bertie followed the haunting sound, cutting across fields, heedless of village dogs baying in competition with the music. Fields gave way to bushes, and soon we came to a row of trees lining the Mandalay–Maymyo Road. Kilt-clad Scots, replete with bagpipes and kettledrums were followed by a large contingent of British soldiers marching abreast. Magnificent in full uniform, they left no doubt they were the victors. A thrill ran up my spine.

The whole village appeared to have turned out, standing on either side of the road. They gaped at the soldiers. Bertie found a place for us in front to watch the march. We skinny, ragged children stood in breathless silence while the stirring sound of martial music filled the valley and resounded over the plains. I gazed through a film of tears. Did these smart soldiers trudge out of Burma, weary and footsore, four long years ago? To my childish eyes, every soldier was a hero.

After a fine display of strength, a sergeant gave the order to halt, and the men set up camp near the village. We overheard the officer-in-charge ask the headman to bring all Anglo-Indians and Anglo-Burmese to meet him, and we ran home to give Mum the good news. The headman sent a messenger to relay the information to Dad. He told us to report to the officer, cautioning Mum not to ask for anything.

Bertie escorted us to the camp and spoke to a sergeant, who pointed to an officer seated on a tree stump. A few soldiers stood guard. Further off, a group of Burmese craned their necks in an effort to catch the conversation. Slim and handsome, the captain wore a moustache like Errol Flynn. When we approached, he stood and shook hands with Mum. He asked whether we needed anything, but Mum said, 'I'm just so happy to see you.'

I wanted to scream, 'We're starving. We need food.' I bit my tongue. Among the villagers who crowded around us were many of dad's relatives who would report every word to him. I was terrified to go against my father.

After the interview, I remained behind with Bertie while Mum returned to the hut with Rose. We stood beneath the shade of a tamarind tree and watched the soldiers operate their guns. The day was hot, and perspiration poured down their shirtless torsos as they worked. I admired their rippling muscles. Gunners milled around the twenty-pounders.

I recalled the newsreels I'd seen so long ago, and I visualised them feeding shells into the guns' iron throats. The guns spat out fire like great dragons. I put my fingers to my ears and chuckled when Bertie told me the men were firing at the Japanese in Mandalay.

That evening, we returned to the hut without a care in the world. Dad had somehow managed to obtain mepacrine tablets for Rupert's malaria, and he was sleeping soundly. By lunchtime the following day, he rose from bed, looking like a ghost. His skin was yellow, and he appeared to have grown taller. Mum placed two buckets of water in the sun for him and, after a hot bath, he joined us for lunch. Rupert ate his share of ox-tail stew and chapatti and licked his lips without taking his eyes off the food. He didn't speak a word, but his appetite had returned, and his indomitable spirit renewed.

Years later, I learned America wanted to reopen the Burma Road to transport military supplies into China to help them fight the Japanese. However, Churchill had been intent on bypassing Burma, and regaining Malaya and Singapore. Fortunately for us, the US president persuaded him to concentrate on Burma first. Because of America's efforts to reconquer northern Burma before the rest of Southeast Asia, Mandalay was liberated by the British after heavy street fighting in March 1945.

If the Allies had postponed retaking Mandalay for a few months, Rupert would surely have died from malaria, cut off in the spring of his life. Many of us would also have succumbed to starvation and sickness.

Rupert survived, despite being dragged off by the Japanese as forced labour, or by being carried off by malaria. I thanked the Lord for saving my brother. Even as a child, it reinforced my belief that though we walk through the valley of death, we should not fear evil. The years of war and Rupert's miraculous escape taught me to always trust the Lord.

Purchase

REVEREND JIM MᶜPHERSON

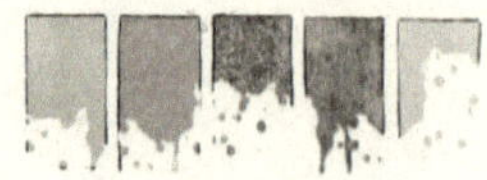

anæsthetised by the purchase
purchase exercises over us

yet: high above the asphalt,
the busy crowds, the traffic blare,

in an air-conditioned world
a two-year-old, with adult help

waters the indoor plants
and feeds the fish-in-glass

mum and dad and little one
all beaming

Secular Trinity

Mercurius will sell you anything, or trade, or buy

Apollos does health care, engineering and much more

Narcissus boasts that Ego conquers all
and died a martyr to his own cause

their purchase on the real no more
        than my foot upon a rock,
            a bird upon the air,
                or a fish upon the water

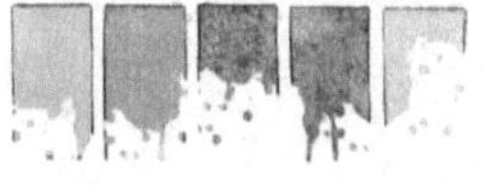

Homo Gaudens

Homo Emptor has no purchase
on the adamantine crust
of Entropy and Time; yet
at Christmas and at birthdays
wistfully enjoys the little ones'
spontaneous, almost volcanic,
surges of innocent delight –
which *Homo Emptor* cannot price
nor *Homo Faber* engineer
nor *Homo Sapiens* fathom

for only rebels who assail the adamantine
crust of everyday, can even hope to join
the Lady Wisdom and her legions of naïfs—
and with them catch the merest glimpse
of the Author's incomparable beauty

The Cage

MIRANDA DE JAGER

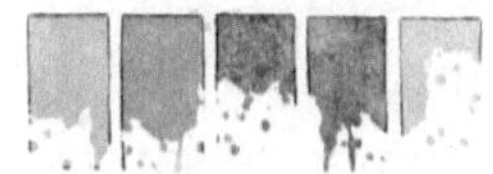

*O*no, not again! I grab the bars and shake them, but they're immovable. I run to the door, push against it, but it's locked. Then I see the padlock on the outside. I slip my hand through the thick bars and lift the padlock. There's no way I'd be able to open it. Tired and dejected, I collapse in the corner of my cage. I am trapped!

I am so tired of this cage. I know I'm talented, I have so much to offer but the cage limits me. I jump up when I see people passing by, I want to shout, but I have no voice. My shouts are like puffs of air escaping from my throat.

They look at me as if everything is normal, but it's not. Can't they see my predicament and the desperation on my face? I want to ask for help, but cannot get the words out. My problem is that I cannot talk. I cannot talk to strangers. I cannot talk in a group; I freeze up completely. It's insane, I know. Other than that, I'm normal—I think. I performed really well at school without studying a great deal. I even obtained a post-graduate degree. Actually, I am good at a lot of things. I have a career, I'm creative, I cook, I sew, I paint, but I cannot talk.

I've always had this problem as far as I can remember. It seems like the cage makes me invisible. People don't even notice me; they don't ask for my opinion and they don't expect me to say anything. I feel like the girl in the movie, *The Princess Diaries*, when someone sat on her at school, because they did not notice her. I'm the invisible onlooker; everybody has accepted it and they seem satisfied with the situation.

As a little girl at school, I was terrible at speeches; I would forget my words and feel my face burning. I had all kinds of nicknames resembling red. Fortunately none of them stuck. Eventually I just wrote down my speeches, and read the whole thing without looking up at anyone. I think the teachers felt so sorry for me that they simply allowed it.

I am stuck in my work too—the cage, of course. Although I'm good at what I do, I realise people who are too shy and withdrawn don't often get promoted. It seems like everybody simply avoids the subject to spare me. It is so embarrassing that I do not have the courage to talk about the fact that I cannot talk. So, in a way, I kind of welcome the fact that nobody mentions it. I may just freeze up again, stuck in this cold hard cage.

You may think: doesn't she know she needs help? Yes, you're right, I know, but the thing is I do not have the courage to ask for help. Who do I ask? What do I say? I may just freeze up again. I have prayed about it so many times. I know God hears my prayers and He has blessed me in many ways. I have a lovely husband and a good life. My prayers are often answered, but somehow I cannot seem to overcome this problem. It's terrible. If you haven't been there, you have no idea what it's like.

Fortunately, I am not entirely spineless. When circumstances drove me into a corner and my cage became even smaller, I finally decided to ask for help. I knew a lovely lady at church who was a trained counsellor. One day I simply walked up to her and asked the dreaded question. I did not freeze up and she took it really well, better than I thought she would. She immediately made an appointment, so it was all set.

The circumstances that caused me to ask the dreaded question was a run-in with my mother. My mother has always been controlling and manipulative. I learned at a very early age that you don't argue with her, it's no use; it's easier to simply agree and do whatever she asks. She had an endless supply of waterproof arguments that made no logical sense to me. Even after I was married, her controlling behaviour did not stop. She would often embarrass me in front of friends or acquaintances. I never suspected a personality disorder. I simply doubted myself, and my confidence plummeted even further. Something deep inside told me that she's wrong, but her arguments were so well-presented that I was left without words. Back to the cage.

D-day finally arrived, and though I'm often late, I was quite early this time. Waiting became so excruciating I simply drove over there to get it over and done with. The counsellor was lovely. She managed to get me to talk and once I started, I couldn't stop. I surprised myself, because I never knew I could talk that much. It was both scary and liberating to be able to talk to someone who was sincere and wanted to help. I needed more sessions and saw her monthly for about a year.

The sessions made me feel lighter and I realised that my mother was not as perfect as she wanted people to believe. After all, nobody's perfect, right? The counselling helped me in many ways. One day when my husband and I were visiting with a group of friends, I started chatting spontaneously. I was amazed at myself because I could never do this before. In that moment I remembered a time I experienced God's touch when the counsellor prayed with me. This was a turning point in my life—my friendships improved and I found communication at work easier.

What I didn't understand was why the cage was still there. I couldn't believe the counsellor was unable to get me out of it. Every time I had a run-in with my mother, or another controlling person, I was stuck in my cage again. Like the time my mother lied when she tried to get her hands on addictive medications. I eventually ran out of her apartment when her lies became unbearable. I just couldn't face it anymore. Back in my cage after shaking the bars, I found my favourite place in the corner and asked: 'Why am I still here after all those months of counselling?' I looked around the cage, the strong bars, the locked door… Wait a minute, where's the padlock?

I jumped up and opened the door—it was unlocked and I was out! I realised that I had to walk out by myself; nobody else could do it for me. I have to stand up to my mother even if my arguments feel lame. The secret is that I can actually talk. I simply have to stand my ground and tell the truth in a polite, firm way.

As time went on, I received professional counselling and suspected that my mother may have Narcissistic Personality Disorder. While she was never diagnosed, because she believed that there was nothing wrong with her, I researched her behaviour. Those investigations confirmed my suspicions and I tried to do whatever I could to help her. I even supported her financially for years after my father died, but she never thanked me or appreciated anything I did. She seemed to care only about herself and would do or say anything to make herself look good—even if she broke someone else down in the process. She never admitted to lying, even when caught red-handed.

The verbal abuse continued until I decided to walk away, knowing I had done everything in my power to salvage our relationship. I continued to pray for her until she died a few years later, after being unable to talk, respond or do anything for herself for many weeks. While it still saddens me, I know that life happens and even when we make mistakes, God loves us and forgives us.

Today, after many years of counselling, I can look back on my life and see how God's grace has saved me. My life could have been so different, my hurt and frustration could have rendered me incapable of making the right choices. I could have made a mess of my life, but my relationship with Jesus and my faith in God gave me perspective. He helped me find a good husband and good friends. He showed me the way in the times when I thought there was no way out.

By the grace of God, I was able to walk away from my cage. I realise that God was always at work in my life, even during the times when it felt like my prayers were unanswered. I found that sometimes God's answers were different from my expectations, He allowed me to go through tough times so I could learn how to handle myself and become more mature in Him. God has never left me alone; He is always close and always has my best interests at heart. I know the cage will never hold me captive again.

God Got Here Long Before Us

JOHN HUGHES

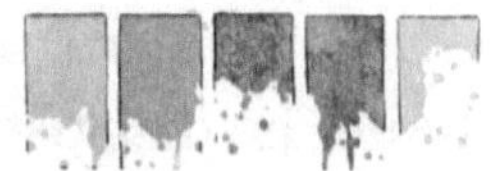

*I*t was an offer he couldn't refuse. Ernie's parole officer had directed him to arrange an appointment. It was hoped my gatekeeper skills could discern a better path in life. But working through his maze of guilt and shame called out for a safe place. It called out for wholehearted listening. It called out for someone—despite potential awkwardness—to commit time, empathy, compassion, and vulnerability. Such encounters are potentially high risk as well as high gain. And they throw appointment schedules into complete disarray.

Ernie was a semi-illiterate man, an Aussie battler willing to take on board the red-letter words found in a stolen Gideon's New Testament. He died homeless in his hand-me-down car. Yet a thin and tenuous garment of faith made him grateful. After all, the Saviour of the World was a homeless man.

I found it easy to warm to Ernie. He was a burly man with a big smile. T-shirt stubbies and thongs were his best suit, low budget tattoos announced his inner turmoil. When his fists were closed, the right hand read 'hate' and the left 'love'. In between attending to his two young boys, Ernie told me his story. He and his partner had been jailed for six months for stealing to support their amphetamine habit. Somehow, the court had arranged sequential sentences for them so they could parent their boys. Now was her time for jail, and Ernie had kicked his habit to be there for the children. But he was edgy. In lowered tones, he disclosed that he was fearful for his own life. As part of a plea bargain, he had provided information to the police about the criminal activities of his drug supplier. While Ernie was street-wise, he was also aware that evil is ruthlessly unpredictable.

With the kids, he was living downstairs in an old Queenslander. His partner's mother lived upstairs and, from the street, the home looked abandoned. Nevertheless, this was a better start for his boys than for his own childhood. Ernie's dad, in good Aussie fashion, drank too much beer. Domestic violence flared and waned. The household was rarely calm. Without parental self-giving love, Ernie became the victim of a sexual predator. It was a lasting trauma. A rape of the image of God in his person. It left a wound that set him up for life. It was to be a hard, hard road.

Understandably, he didn't engage with schooling and, after recurrent visits to the principal's office, Ernie slipped through the cracks in the education system to specialise in street skills. He was barely literate, but made his way by observing human behaviour. He learnt to be practical and effective with his hands.

At 15, another tragedy fragmented his world. His older brother suicided. As well as personally distressing, this was a painful eruption of his family's unhealthy life. His mother was grief-stricken. Sins against us can carry an overwhelming burden of shame. In this darkness, we lose sight of God who makes clothes to cover over shame. We groan.

Prior to his time in jail, Ernie had also survived the terror of a home invasion. He was woken from sleep by attackers who menaced him to extort perceived drug money debts. Death became a backdrop—a game of musical chairs as Ernie battled to resist his own thoughts of suicide and the ever-present threat of evil. Every evening ushered in a long, dark night of his soul.

During this first encounter, we had somehow successfully kicked the can down the road together. A relationship was established. It didn't take long before Ernie's physical health took centre stage, and his trust was tested. His burly frame covered up a brewing metabolic syndrome. Laced with nicotine and a thoughtless diet, Ernie found himself in hospital with an acute coronary syndrome. He survived, but his weight was seen as a problem. Any intervention to improve his prospects was deferred until he lost a lot of this excess.

Systems can often be indifferent to the needs of individuals. Ernie was a young man, the father of two young children. From every angle, the odds were stacked against him. At these times, gatekeepers look for another way. I advocated for help at another facility where weight was not a barrier. Ernie had the biggest smile on his face as he told of two stents inserted to open out his blocked coronary arteries. Staff had been kind. He bit the bullet and stopped smoking. Little did he know his health challenges were just warming up.

As a primary care doctor, I have the privilege of sitting on the same side of the table with people whose lives are complex. Health is a mosaic of biological, perinatal, and subsequent life context stressors, psychological strengths and weaknesses, social and family dysfunction mixed in with some good—all along with the flickers of the Spirit, of the image of God in each one of us. Against most measures, my life is good. It's only when I sit on the same side of the table with people like Ernie, people who give full voice to the old spiritual, *Nobody Knows The Trouble I've Seen*, that my own repressed hurts and struggles, my own blind spots, come into view. Those memories and wounds that nobody knows but Jesus! The danger is that I grip Jesus as my own, rather than standing in solidarity with the deep love of Jesus for the Ernies of this world.

On one hand, Christians hold an awareness that God has a special concern for people who are poor, 'disposable', broken-hearted—people at the margins of the world's life. On the other hand, I am amazed, perhaps even outraged, that a substantial cohort of people live from within a constant stream of misery. For some, this is the consequence of their own choices—but mostly it is the impact of the sins of others. More broadly, it follows from injustice.

In time, Ernie's problems became a litany of suffering. He developed a chronic painful, malodourous pilonidal sinus, an infection between his buttocks. His partner, now back in the community, called the shots and Ernie was suddenly out in the couch-surfing world, looking for a bed for the night. I convinced him to take a sleep study. This was strongly positive for obstructive sleep apnoea. A loud, snoring, big, smelly man is not a good candidate as a long-term boarder.

At hospital, the surgeons made an attempt to excise this festering flesh. Almost predictably, the surgery broke down, leaving a more severe and painful chronic sinus. Bucketloads of antibiotics were required and a new threatening health problem emerged in the form of diabetes. Ernie never came to terms with diabetes. At one point, he became so ill he was hospitalised in intensive care with a keto-acidosis crisis. Insulin was hit-and-miss and, in due course, a numbness of his feet wrapped itself in place. Troublesome feet infection became part of the story as Ernie was welded to his thongs. These provided little protection under the new circumstances.

Mental health and relationship fronts also carried dark clouds. Twice, he failed to hang himself and, on another occasion, he was restrained and hospitalised for attempting to jump in front of a train. This occurred after breaking up with a new girlfriend. In his mind, Ernie had fallen in love, but drug misuse—again—exposed his underlying anger. The woman moved to regional Queensland and, in desperation, Ernie followed. Eventually, he got the message when her son beat him up. Things were looking bleak for Ernie, even at his most likeable moments.

The apostle James encourages his downtrodden friends with the words, *'Is any one of you suffering? He should pray.'* (James 5:13 BSB) I started to pray for Ernie. I brought his name forward at prayer meetings on occasion. I held onto hope for him.

Science is black-and-white when it comes to exposure to domestic violence, childhood sexual abuse, and traumatic grief. It is bad for both physical and mental health outcomes. If the cognitive daze of untreated obstructive sleep apnoea is thrown over all this, as in Ernie's case, the light at the end of the tunnel of suffering almost disappears.

Brené Brown[1] is a Harvard professor who researches shame, courage and vulnerability. She has written a number of helpful books from this vantage. She defines shame as 'the intensely painful feeling or experience of believing we are flawed and therefore unworthy of love and belonging.' We are becoming very aware from exploring the experience of domestic violence, sexual abuse and other trauma that shame is close to the surface for many of us. Ernie lived the reality of a shame-based depleted self. Men, according to Brown, interpret shame as failure, weakness, of being ridiculed, and showing fear. This self-narrative leads to anger and withdrawal. Ernie's anger flared in relationships, particularly when love was at stake. So, most of the time, he withdrew either to a false happy-go-lucky persona (he dyed his hair green and wore strange clothes for a while), or to his car, his substitute home. Moreover, Brown suggests there are three common defence mechanisms or armour that people living with shame take on board:

(1) foreboding joy or dread—perhaps indicated by Ernie's fear of violent assault

(2) perfectionism—I don't think Ernie went down this path; his diabetes would have been much better managed if he had, and

(3) numbing—undoubtedly a strong driver for his drug misuse.

While chronic oppressive shame is a driver for anxiety and depression, the courage to heal starts with a willingness to become vulnerable. That is, for a person to own their own story of shame, and take steps of courage to reach out. Ernie, to some extent, was pushed into vulnerability by his parole officer. My role was to consciously open a door of welcome, both as a health professional and in the Spirit of Jesus.

Over the long haul, this was enough to allow an appreciation of beauty—seen through cracks in his armour. Cracks that allowed for the light of Christ to shine through. From time to time, Ernie found his way back to visit me at my practice. There were matters to attend to: scripts to write, forms to reapply for housing support, and of course an obligatory pep talk about his diabetes care.

---

1 Brown, B. (2015). *Daring greatly: How the courage to be vulnerable transforms the way we live, love, parent, and lead.* Penguin.

One day, I noticed what I suspected was a Gideon's New Testament in his shirt pocket. Ernie confirmed my suspicion, and proudly announced he had 'stolen it'. He could see I was temporarily lost for words, so he continued, 'The red-letter words are good, aren't they?' He may have offered his diversion to cut off any reaction to his recidivism.

'You stole it?' I responded with bemusement. Ernie's big smile got me in and I asked, 'Do you know whose words are the ones in red?'

Reading was always a challenge, but a level of excitement accompanied Ernie's response when I told him it was Jesus.

'Jesus, fair dinkum?' came straight from his heart.

'Yep, fair dinkum indeed.'

We agreed Jesus was pretty good when He spoke in the stories. They are words worth reading and Ernie committed to this difficult task. I couldn't resist the challenge and recommended to Ernie that Jesus wasn't into stealing and would encourage him to change his ways. We laughed and moved on.

Professional space doesn't privilege time to talk about gospel stories. Yet the transformative healing that can come as anyone encounters the voice of Jesus is relevant to everyone. Ernie would report in from time to time. He seemed to be taking his reading to heart. Then, one day, he lost his electronic car key. Ernie had poured his practical, creative best into fitting out his mobile car home, but this was a crisis. It forced a downsizing and a return to couch-surfing. Somehow, he fell into cash-in-the-hand work with a farmer, and this helped scrape together enough money for a new, barely roadworthy vehicle. Necessity is the mother of invention and he set to the task to reestablish home. Hygiene wasn't great, but he would shower in public facilities scattered here and there, and lived from day to day. Petrol was expensive, he would remind me.

I sensed a new hope in his voice when he shared the possibility of moving into a flat with the son. This hope was overtaken by further health issues. After more than a decade, an opportunity for surgery for his chronic pilonidal sinus came up. Patience is needed if you are poor. I had mentioned generally over time that I would pray for Ernie in his struggles. This important operation felt threatening, so I offered more specifically to pray at this time. He issued a grateful response. It felt like now or never.

With the operation going well, it meant he was back into his car. The weather was moderate and during one conversation for advice and medication, Ernie disclosed he had found a drop-in centre where he could shower, get a feed, and enjoy conversation. 'These Christian people are pretty good,' he testified. 'They are good to talk to, they respect me.'

'It sounds like Jesus is getting through to you,' I mused.

'I don't want any church stuff,' he responded, 'but, yeah, this is good.'

Advocacy was an action that Ernie warmed to. He was always vulnerable to new episodes of shame and humiliation. In this regional centre, he found himself quite ill with abdominal pain. Acute diverticular disease saw him hospitalised, requiring intravenous antibiotics. He had recently started to smoke cigarettes again, and most of the nurses allowed Ernie to march his drip and stand to the hospital footpath for an occasional smoke.

One day, a very assertive nurse challenged him. When Ernie tried to plead his case, she shouted, called security, and he was instantly discharged. Still not well, he gathered his few things and was escorted out of hospital. Not long after, he spilled bleach on his right foot. Thongs were no protection, and with little feeling because of his diabetic neuropathy, this foot became badly infected. He attended a local clinic. The after-hours doctor started an IV line with antibiotics as the foot infection was now nasty. When Ernie was advised to go to the regional hospital for possible surgery, he panicked and refused. Without further encouragement, an angry doctor removed the drip and Ernie was unceremoniously evicted by security once again. It was cold and wet outside, and he was toxic.

All my medical instincts were telling me this was bad medical care. Ernie needed help quickly to prevent the amputation of toes, or even his whole foot. A letter of complaint to the regional hospital superintendent, and strong urging for Ernie to try again for help, saw a decent care plan developed. Ernie transferred to a major metropolitan hospital. His foot was saved.

Sometime ago, I remember watching a John Wayne Western. There were no academy awards for this serving of spaghetti, but a short piece of the dialogue stuck with me. One of the riders was complaining bitterly about the God-forsaken wilderness around them. The hero, Wayne, surveyed the desolation and dryly responded, 'God got here long before us.'

Many people would look at another's life journey and assign 'God-forsaken' to it. With eyes to see and ears to hear, a second good look will always be to the contrary.

A few months down the track again, I was on the phone for a telehealth call about another flare of diverticular disease. Ernie's diet not only fuelled his diabetes and metabolic syndrome, but contributed to this bowel dysfunction. After clarifying his symptoms, sending off an e-script for antibiotics, and discussing a pending surgical appointment to remove the damaged bowel, Ernie became surprisingly reflective. He began to disclose a growing awareness of God's goodness to him personally. He talked about his successful surgery, the unexpected work to buy his next car—his homebase—and also the relational joy he'd experienced with drop-in centre friends. 'I am really grateful God cares for me,' he summarised.

My quiet affirmation was: 'You never know where God's goodness will take you.' We continued to reflect in silence.

'All good, all good,' Ernie concluded.

God was touching his heart, but I needed to keep my professional distance.

I missed the next call for his scripts and arrived at work intending to follow it up. My eagerness soon evaporated. The reception staff team were sombre as they let me know Ernie had been found dead in his car. He had passed alone during the night in his mobile 'home'. Soon, I was on the phone talking to a police officer about issuing a death certificate. Then I sighed.

Death is always a bittersweet experience. Life itself is a great gift. For Ernie, suffering and sorrow accompanied him throughout his life. There is no glamour in suffering. To a small extent, I had 'walked a mile and shared the load' with Ernie. His life has been a gift—a glimpse of God's grace over time to me. Ernie battled with fear that someone with evil intent would take his life at any moment. His own life trajectory with its biological, social and family vulnerabilities led him into a constant wrestle with himself. Should he take his own life? God's grace touched him in simple ways.

His own thin garment of faith was made for him by another homeless man who died on a Roman Cross and rose to lead sons like Ernie to glory.

Through the Lens of Grace

LINDA BARTON

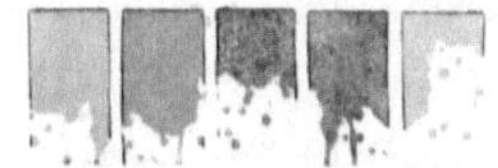

'The cataclysm has happened, we are among the ruins, we start to build up new little habits, to have new little hopes. It is rather hard work: there is no smooth road into the future: but we go round, or we scramble over the obstacles. We've got to live, no matter how many skies have fallen in.'

DH Lawrence

The words echo off the page and I am transported through the long lens of history back to that veranda on the old farmhouse fifty years past. It is dark. The dark you only get when you are far from civilisation. The pre-dawn witching hour. And there I am, a child of seven years of age, amongst the ruins.

The light from the kitchen door spills out across the veranda, splitting the darkness with its yellow incandescence and bathing my mother with its soft glow. She looks like a lone actress numbed by stage fright as the policeman's torchlight skipped across the shadows.

I rub my hand across my weary eyes and feel the grittiness scratch under my lids. My tongue is dry and swollen as I run it across my teeth, furry from the lack of brushing and the lingering aftertaste of stale milk from the bedtime Milo Mother made me hours ago. My sister, Debbie, one year my junior, is standing beside me and looking dishevelled and bleary-eyed. I wonder if I look as confused as she does as we stand with our backs against the wall of the house—as if the solidity of the timber building will offer us some measure of protection. Ground us in reality. No, this is not a dream—it is real.

My two older sisters and brother are huddled together by the railing and looking down at the police officers. They will know what is happening and understand. They will know our father has died in a car accident and won't be coming home. Not this morning—or any other morning. Never again.

I don't know this and I can't understand what is being said. All I can hear is the low rumble, like distant thunder, as the policeman speaks. I watch and wait. It must be bad, as Mother has not told us to go back to bed. In fact, it appears she does not even know we are there. It's as if her world stops at the edge of the spray of light.

How long did we stand there? How long before the police left in their car with the cherry red light on top? Who put us back to bed? All irrelevant and inconsequential when your whole world has crashed and the universe has splintered.

It is only from this distance, light years from the event, that I fully understand the cataclysmic and far-reaching consequences of that terrible night. I am unsure now, with the dimming of memory and the many skies that have fallen since, how I felt following my father's death. The shadow of my mother's grief and the enormity of the path that lay before us perhaps overshadows all other emotions. Mother was left widowed, with a brood of seven children ranging in age between 3 and 12 years. She was now the sole income earner and owner of a small cropping farm with no skills beside motherhood to see her through. She had no driver's licence—or even a car now—and lived a half hour drive from the nearest shops. A mountain of obstacles to scramble over with young children in tow.

Like all memories, mine are piecemeal. They flick from one scene to the next—a newsreel with three-second motion picture snippets, capturing a lifetime. The highs, bright and cheery, and the lows, sharp and painful—all to be examined with care. They can still draw blood. Some just random pictures, I can't even place sequentially anymore.

Thanks so much, DH Lawrence, I think, not without sarcasm. *Now you've opened a can of worms and there is no going back.*

The reel plays on and flicks to a new scene. I am tucked up in the double bed with my little sister in the room I also share with two of my other siblings. It is dark and late at night. Debbie is snuggled up against me, her soft breath on my cheek. I roll on my side towards the window to give myself a little space and hopefully not disturb her. The full moon lights up the room and I can see my brothers sound asleep. I am the sole beneficiary of the concert in progress, as the night choir sings me their lullaby.

The frogs and the crickets are harmonising, *a cappella*, while the curlews take the gong for singing out of tune.

In the background, I can hear my mother. She is also awake. But the beauty of the night is not for her eyes and ears this evening. I hear her muffled weeping. She buries her sorrow in her sheets and sheds her tears for my father and for herself in the dark. I know when morning comes, she will be busy, the captain in command of the troops, ordering and delegating to ensure our lives move on despite there being no smooth road into the future.

Flick. Granddad is here again this afternoon. Time for mother to have another driving lesson. She is anxious. I can tell. She is sharp and cutting with her words and it is a good time to be elsewhere or about your chores. Preferably with fervour, even if it's the dreaded toilet clean. When they return, mother will be tired and there will be a bag of lollies to share.

Flick. Multiple images coalesce into a single frame.

Mother has lost most of her hair. It disappeared over a period of time. Strand by strand. It is not funny. Mother is a small framed woman with a proportionally small heart-shaped face. The look is elfin: sad and bedraggled. For a woman who has always taken particular pride in her looks, particularly her hair and dress, it is distressing not only for her but for us all. Yes! It is worrying. Mother is not coping.

Flick. A picture begins to form, much as a photographic image swims into focus in a darkroom. Mother has a wig. We are all intrigued. It looks exactly like her own hair in colour and texture. Even the tight curls are consistent with her pre-catastrophe hairdo. It has pride of place on her dressing table. We are not allowed to touch it.

Flick. The pictorial record spins the narrative on to a single snapshot image. Time is inconsequential and nonsequential as we rush forward along this memory stream. My brothers, sisters and I have just arrived home from school, after a long walk home from the bus stop. We enter the kitchen to find a stranger sitting at the table with Mother. They are having afternoon tea. The table is laid with a fresh cloth and the best tea service is in use. Homemade cake and biscuits are arranged on a plate in its centre.

The man appears to be relaxed and at ease, as if he has been here many times before. He is dressed in a black suit with a white shirt and tie. Mother is dressed in her town clothes, her new wig, brushed and styled, is also firmly in place. Who is this man? What is he doing here? Childhood confusion. What happened next? Were we introduced? Did Mother explain? Is this the reason for the new wig? The details are a blur. This would not be the last time this man would appear in our lives. We did not know it at the time, but his appearance in our mother's life would have a profound impact and change her life forever.

Flick. Multiple images superimposed simultaneously transposing time, space and emotion. The juxtaposition of montage compelling me to search for the meaning behind this particular sequence of images.

I am in my best dress this morning. I hate dresses, particularly ones that are frilly and starched. I give it a good beating on the end of my bed before putting it on, but the frill around the top is still itching my neck. Mother keeps telling me to stop fussing and be still and quiet. I am too excited though and full of restless energy. We have not been out as a family for a long time.

I am at the local community hall with Mother and my siblings. The hall is essentially a corrugated shed without any internal walls, lining or ceiling. The building is on stumps with steps that lead into the wide-open space. The floor is wooden planks with wooden bench seating circling the internal perimeter of the building. We used to go here on a Saturday night to the old-time dances as a family with father. Music, dancing, billy tea and, best of all, sandwiches and cake—even for the children.

But today is Sunday, and the stranger that comes to afternoon tea with Mother is here too, along with many other local families. We sit on the hard wooden bench in our family groups. The stranger—Mother's stranger—seems to have some power and influence in this space. Like the conductor of an orchestra, he determines the tempo and melody of the proceedings—the ups and downs of the participants, the music, the words and the silences. I am confused and a little annoyed. There is no dancing or yummy food.

Mother is shushing me and batting at my hand when I try to smooth down my frill. At one stage during the proceedings, a bowl is passed around and people put money on the plate which then is placed on the piano. According to the stranger, God lives here and the money is for Him. Our family had not been practising Christians or ever attended the local church services prior to this time, so the rituals and procedures were alien and nonsensical.

This is the first of many Sundays spent in the company of the parish church minister and the members of that Christian community. Mother had found God. Or did God find Mother? As I step out of the childhood frame back into myself, while I am not sure who found who, I do know with the hindsight of history that it has been her salvation. The minister's regular visits to our home following my father's death, by the grace of God and the minister's compassion, helped her find hope and healing and the strength to navigate a path forward for herself and our family.

Now, as Mother nears the horizon on her life, she continues to lean into her faith for sustenance and comfort. She is almost 90 years of age and is legally blind, but still lives alone and attends church regularly. Her journey to salvation has not always been easy. It has involved sacrifice and self-denial.

However, Mother's belief is steadfast and she is adamant that the choice to follow the course chartered by God's will has been the best and most rewarding decision she made in her life.

AUTHORS

DONNA ALBRECHT

Donna began writing her testimony in 2017 after a series of God-given prompts. Her first story was published in *Stories of Life Anthology* in 2018, and short-listed for *Eternity Matters: Short Stories of Life*. She continues to stretch her writing muscles, hoping to share more stories of God's transforming power. She lives in Queensland with her husband and 3 rebellious chooks.

HAZEL BARKER

Hazel was born in Burma of an Iranian Muslim father and an English Catholic mother. Blacklisted by the Burmese Junta, she fled to Australia, where her heart's desires were fulfilled when she married the boy of her dreams. Her short stories, memoirs and literary novels have won many awards. Three were finalists in the Australia and New Zealand CALEB Competitions of 2017, 2019 and 2022, respectively.

LINDA BARTON

Based on her mother's true story, Linda Barton wrote *Through the Lens of Grace*, a poignant short story that depicts how a young child witnessed her mother's struggle and triumph over adversity and discovered her faith. Linda is a practising Christian and enjoys creative writing, hiking, and bird watching. She lives with her husband and their rescued animals on a small hobby farm in Toowoomba.

RUTH BONETTI

Stories of real people, past and present, fascinate Ruth Bonetti. Her career in classical music became a passport to the world. Destiny led her to Sweden and Finland where she researched her grandfather's story, and that of the black-sheep brother who in 1899 dodged conscription into the Russian army–pursued to Suez. Her award-winning *Midnight Sun to Southern Cross* trilogy (historical biography/memoir) includes *The Art Deco Mansion in St Lucia*. Ruth's music, education and performance publications include two with Oxford University Press. Ruth founded Omega Writers in 1991.

ROSS CLARK

Ross is the author of nine published volumes of poetry, and the recipient of awards including the Peter Porter Poetry Prize. He also writes and performs folken-country-blues songs (solo or with a band). In addition his haiku are published in a number of countries. If pressed, he will describe (not define) himself as a zen Anglican. And warn of further volumes ready for publication.

DIANA DAVISON

Diana lives in Brisbane, Queensland. Her work has appeared in *Poetry* anthologies, *Stories of Life* short stories, *Grieve* Hunter Writers Centre anthologies here in Australia and a small scattering of publications overseas. She remains inspired by nature, family and the constant changes life presents.

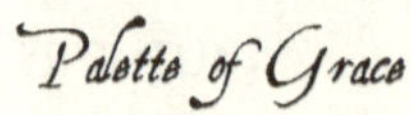

MIRANDA DE JAGER

Miranda grew up in South Africa where childhood challenges cultivated her passion to overcome hardship and encourage others. She started working at eighteen, obtained a degree while working full time and pursued an IT career. Miranda and her husband moved to Brisbane in 2010 and became Australian Citizens four years later. Miranda is fond of reading and enjoys anything creative, including sewing, painting and writing poetry.

M. LESTER DIGHTON

Bishop M. Lester Dighton was born and raised in Queensland in a Humanistic environment with strong occult influences. While conducting various occult studies himself, he had an encounter with God which completely changed his life. He is now a self-supported Evangelical Preacher, who works individually with small groups and people in need in a variety of ways, and is a Chaplain to those whom he can serve.

TERRY GATFIELD

Born under the sound of Bow Bells when the Luftwaffe was decimating the London landscape. Came to Brisbane at the dawn of the hippie movement. Tamed by one wife and four wonderful children plus their delightful 10 offspring. Taught at various universities, collected a handful of degrees. Travelled Asia, learnt Chinese. Published and conferenced about 100 papers. Retired now in a blissful ecological environment to play the flute and write the occasional book.

ANNE HAMILTON

Anne was a mathematics teacher for 30 years before she decided one day it possibly wasn't her calling. She then realised she'd better apply for some jobs just to practise her interview skills. The first position she tried for was at Vision Christian Media and she was appointed the Australian editor of the well-known devotionals, *The Word for Today* and *Vision180*. She is the award-winning author of over 30 books.

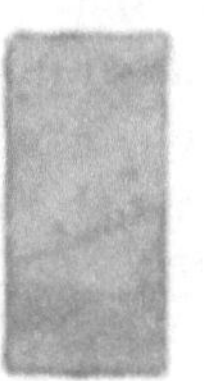

LYNDA HAMMOND

Lynda has over thirty years of ministry experience and currently serves on the Pastoral Team at Dalby Christian Family Church

Lynda carries a prophetic teaching gift and has authored five books, including a devotional on Exodus, a Bible study around personal renewal, and three devotional books with lessons drawn from life experience. Her passion is to see a generation rise up to take their place in selfless faith.

JOHN HUGHES

'John Hughes' is a pseudonym for a medical practitioner. The names of his patients in these stories have been changed to protect their identities. John enjoys the work of applying best practice care skills in a relational environment and understands that Jesus always stands between himself and his patients. This can lead to unexpected calls for compassion and respect. Reflecting and writing about this work is an emerging joy.

PAMELA JULIAN

As a non-fiction writer, Pamela finds the joy and struggles of life experience provide a rich resource for writing from a faith-based perspective. She has had a number of devotions, life stories and poems published in various anthologies. This year is a return to writing, and includes a potential venture into fiction. Pamela has a background of working in health and disability. She enjoys gardening, and a good book.

JIM MCPHERSON

Jim McPherson has served in the Dioceses of Canberra-Goulburn, of Sydney, and of Brisbane. He was Principal of St Francis Theological College in Brisbane in the 1990s, and he retired from St Paul's Maryborough in 2014. He has published two poetry collections, *To Tease Our Knowing* and *The Gravity of Odd*. He has a science background and a quirky sense of humour. He and his wife Marcia live in Mt Coolum, and belong to Holy Spirit Anglican Church, Coolum.

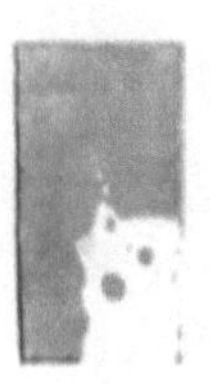

ROSEMARY NEW

Rosemary's country childhood was lonely, with books for companions, and imaginary friends for concocting adventure!

Her first story was written at age seven, about a naughty kitten, bound into an eight-page book with dressmaking pins. Proudly shown to her teacher, who underlined the two spellings mistakes with red pen (which blotted her creative writing for over 30 years) until Rosemary was flabbergasted when God said, *"I want you to write a book."*

That book and a novel are in process. She has one other anthology published story, *Simply Simon* 2016.

JUDY ROGERS

Judy is a retired primary Special Education teacher. She is also a leadership Trainer volunteering with Girl Guides Queensland. Judy enjoys gardening, painting, travelling and spending time with her children, ten grandchildren and two spoilt puppies.

These stories of grace and redemption are a little different from her usual genre of early high school fantasy.

JO WANMER

Jo Wanmer writes to tell of the wonderful things God has done. Her first book was written to display God's work in her life. You will find it hidden in the fiction story, *Though the Bud be Bruised*. These short stories are also written to display God's grace and wonder.

EMELY WEILER

Emely Rose Weiler was born in Germany in 2012. In 2016, she moved to Australia with her parents and her younger brother. Emely and her brother are home-schooled by their parents. Apart from her love to read and write stories, Emely is passionate about playing the violin, the piano and singing. She loves animals, cooking and sports. She is a junior lifesaver and a good tennis player.